Forever, Please

Other Titles by Willow Summers

Jessica Brodie Diaries

Back in the Saddle, Book 1

Hanging On, Book 2

A Wild Ride, Book 3

Growing Pains Series

Lost and Found, Book 1

Overcoming Fear, Book 2

Butterflies in Honey, Book 3

Growing Pains Boxed Set (books 1-3)

Love and Chaos, Cassie's Story

Love Series

Surviving Love

Conquering Love

Forever, Please

BY
WILLOW SUMMERS

Contact info:
Website: WillowSummers.com
Email: info@willowsummers.com

Chapter 1

———— ❧ ————

"COME IN HERE." Hunter passed by my desk with a determined stride. His palm slapped the door, pushing it wide as he went into his office.

I looked over at Brenda with comically wide eyes and a thin mouth. "Sounds like I'm in trouble…"

"I'll say. What'd you do?"

I got up and grabbed my notepad, just in case the bad mood wasn't directed at me. I didn't have high hopes. "Not sure."

"Close the door," Hunter said as I made my way toward him.

A thrill arrested me. My breath quickened. Since moving in with him two months ago, we hadn't partaken in much office fornication. He usually just left work earlier and went home with me. He wanted to take his time. I was all for being bent over the desk, though. Since finding out I was pregnant, he'd been too gentle by half. I needed a good rogering.

"You wanted to see me?" I asked with a grin. I stood

beside his desk.

"Sit." He leaned his elbows against the desk. The light from the windows behind him showered his broad shoulders. His sexy, hooded eyes trained on me. I marveled at his handsome face, with its strong jaw, straight nose, and lush lips.

I was the luckiest girl in the world to be able to kiss those lips. To feel his firm touch and reap the benefits of his clever fingers. There was a list a mile long of girls that wanted him, but he'd chosen me. I didn't have to understand why; I just had to bask in the glory.

"Your game goes live tomorrow, right?" Hunter asked, his gaze dipping for a brief moment, touching my stomach. "Come here."

"I—huh?"

He stood and reached for me. "Come here and sit on my lap."

I smiled like an idiot. I bounced up and grabbed his hand. He reeled me in before sitting on his chair and settling me onto his lap. His lips grazed my neck as his palm covered my belly. "How are you?"

I laughed with the change in his tone. "I'm good. Kind of tired. The baby blogs say that's normal, though."

"That's what I wanted to talk to you about. You're doing too much. You have shadows under your eyes and you're dragging."

I tensed. "Hunter, I haven't had much choice. We had the final push for the app these last few weeks. We're good now, though. The marketing is all set up, the game is loaded, the bugs are worked out—we're ready. Now I can relax."

"Bruce says you have another project coming up. You have more levels to design for this game…"

I got off his lap. I couldn't help my testy tone. "You're my boss in this job, Hunter. You're not my boss with the side project."

"It's my job to look after you and our baby, Olivia. You're doing too much. It has to end."

I snatched up my notepad. He'd been saying this for the last few weeks. Over and over he harped on about the amount of work I was doing, but at the same time, most of it was for him. By the time I finished all of his tasks, it was late. Then I could do what I loved, which was working for Bruce. In order to break this cycle, I had to choose. One job or the other. Hunter knew it, Bruce knew it, and, unfortunately, I knew it too.

The problem was that the one that paid well, and was with the man I loved, didn't interest me. My favorite part of the day was working on Bruce's projects. Most of the new levels were my design. Bruce was starting to step away a little to come up with the next great thing while I took on the future of the current game. I even had an idea for a game of my own.

I shook my head and started for the door.

"Olivia." The deep, commanding voice dripped down my spine and pooled in my lady parts. I slowed despite myself. I loved when he used that tone. It did things to my body that should be illegal.

I turned to him, raising my eyebrows in a silent question.

"I love you. Good luck tomorrow." He turned to his computer.

Warmth spread throughout my chest. My heart surged.

I left the office, wondering where my irritation at his talk had gone. The man could knock me off balance way too easily.

"Did you get in trouble?" Brenda asked as I sat down.

"Kinda. Same old thing—I work too much."

"That's rich, coming from him."

"I know, right?" I scoffed. I'd found my irritation again. "He works more now than before—" I snapped my mouth shut. I was about to say "before I got pregnant." That was a big no-no. All the blogs and books said it was best not to tell anyone before the three-month point, when the chance of miscarriage dropped significantly. Besides that, I wasn't married, hadn't known Hunter that long, and didn't have one thing in my future figured out. There were more than a few reasons not to spread the news around yet.

"What is he doing so late, anyway?" I asked as I turned to my computer. "I tried to spy on him, but his calendar is locked up tight."

"He had me block it off for structural organization. Probably trying to fit the pieces of that new company into this one."

"Huh." I squinted at my company email. Seeing that nothing new had come in, I checked my personal email on my phone. Three new messages, all from Bruce.

"What was that sigh for?" Brenda was facing her computer.

"You're nosy."

"You're more interesting than my job."

I read the first message, then the second, then rolled my eyes on the third. "Bruce is just as demanding as Hunter. He wants me to complete a bio for our website."

"You have a website? What's it called? I wanna look."

"It's not live yet. For a guy who just sold his business, Bruce is hellbent on jumping right back into the fire."

"At least you like the work."

I couldn't argue with that.

I pulled up the report I was supposed to be working on, but my brain kept sliding sideways. First it would go to Bruce's emails. Then I'd think about the game I wanted to design until my thoughts returned to the baby.

It wasn't just me using this body anymore.

Holy crap, I'm pregnant!

I worked on hiding my smile. If Brenda randomly glanced over and saw it, she'd ask what I was so happy about. Being happy was sometimes a personal affront to her mood.

I still couldn't believe it. I was going to have a baby. With Hunter Carlisle! Karma was shining on me; that was for sure. I didn't even care that he'd gotten way overprotective. Given his past, he was forgiven.

Letting a small smile curl my lips, I tried again to focus on my work.

AT EIGHT O'CLOCK I rolled my shoulders and sat back, totally drained. My eyelids drooped and my body felt completely depleted. This growing a human thing was taxing on the energy front, I'd say that much.

I took a deep breath, checked my phone, but ignored the little red button on my email. I'd bet those six messages were all from Bruce. The man couldn't consolidate. He'd think of something, fire off an email, think of something else a moment later, and fire off another. Apparently a notepad for ideas leading to a summary was too much to ask.

I walked into Hunter's office. When he noticed me, he glanced at the clock at the top of his desk. His lips turned into a thin line.

"Don't say anything," I warned. Not waiting for an invitation, I walked directly to him and draped myself across his lap. I flung my arms around his shoulders and buried my face into his neck. "It won't help."

"How much work do you still have to do?"

"For you, or for Bruce?"

He paused. "This isn't working, Olivia. We agreed to stop working so much when we had a family. Our family starting quickly doesn't negate the need to slow down."

"I have six months to slow down. Let's just get this release out of the way, and then I'll have less to do. A couple more days and I'm in the clear."

"What do you have to do for Bruce tonight?" he asked as he softly ran his fingertips down my back. His hands pulled on my silk blouse, untucking the ends from my skirt. His palms ran up the bare skin of my back.

"Little things, I think. By the time you're done here, I'll be done."

"I might be late. I have a couple meetings."

"I didn't see any on your calendar…"

His fingers glided over my bra strap. A quick tightening and then my bra loosened. His hand slid over my skin until he reached up and cupped a breast.

I moaned as my nipple tightened under his palm.

"I'm just trying to square everything away. I foresee a few late nights hammering out a new direction for the company."

I let my head fall back as he kneaded my breast. "Does that brain ever shut off?"

His lips traced a trail of heat up my neck. "How are you feeling?"

"If you're asking if I'm feeling good enough to bend over your desk, I absolutely am."

His hand dropped to between my thighs. I spread my legs as my breath quickened. His fingers traced down the middle of my sex before pushing aside my panties. He rubbed in the right spot.

"Oh, Hunter." I put pressure on his chin, turning his head my way. I nibbled his lips as a digit worked into my body. My core wound up, needing him.

I put my palm on his cheek and deepened the kiss.

My tongue flirted with his as his finger sped up. His thumb worked lazy circles around my clit.

"Oh." I sighed against his lips, gyrating clumsily while still on his lap. His pace quickened, rubbing and thrusting. My body started to burn. My moans intensified.

"Oh, God. I'm going to—" My words cut off in a hasty release of breath. Shivers racked my body as pleasure coursed through me, setting me on fire. I spasmed with the climax before melting in his lap.

After I'd come down, Hunter stood me up gently. His body pushed against mine, trapping me against the desk. His kiss became insistent as his palms worked up the outside of my thighs, lifting my skirt. I wrapped my arms around his neck, lost in the kiss. In the feel of him.

He turned me around. A palm in the middle of my back had me bending. I heard his belt jingle, and then felt his blunt tip against my opening.

"Hmm," I said as my eyes fluttered closed.

That tip applied pressure, parting my folds. I braced, expectant. His hard length entered me slowly, so large. The breath rushed out of my lungs, everything focused on the searing pleasure that worked into my body.

"Yes, Hunter." I bent over further, wanting more.

His chest lay against my back as his hips met my skin. He held himself inside me before backing out slowly.

"Faster," I begged.

He complied. With a hard thrust, he entered me

completely. I moaned, pushed against the desk.

"Let me know if this is uncomfortable," he said softly, his voice shaking slightly.

He pumped into me again, and then again, his movements becoming frantic. I braced against the desk, my eyes closed, as pleasure ran through me in waves. My core, already warmed up, was now in overdrive, soaking up each thrust in ecstasy.

"Yes, Hunter," I said. I gripped the edge of the wood, focused on that pounding pleasure. On the friction. On his body inside mine. "Oh, yes."

I rocked my hips in tiny movements, adding just that bit more. The feelings now overwhelming. The sensations pulling me under.

"Oh God. Oh my God. Oh—" Everything tightened up. My toes curled.

"Oh!" I blasted apart. Intense wave after wave rocked through me. The orgasm stole my breath as Hunter quaked over me.

His hands slid down my arms. His fingers threaded through mine as we came down, panting over the desk.

"I promised myself I'd be more careful with you," he whispered.

I turned my face toward him until his lips were glancing off my cheek. "The human body isn't that fragile, Hunter."

"Still. I don't want anything to go wrong, Olivia. I don't want you or the baby put in any kind of danger."

If I wasn't mistaken, there was a tiny plea in his

voice. His past was trying to encroach on this conversation, I had no doubt.

I straightened up. I knew a moment of regret when his body left mine—something that never seemed to go away—before I turned around and put my arms around his neck. "I'm good. I need a little bump and grind every so often."

He gave me a lingering kiss. "Okay, off you get." He helped me straighten up my clothes. "I don't want you awake when I get home. You need your rest."

"What time are you coming home?"

"A couple hours, I think."

I gave him a flat look. "That's more than a twelve-hour day, Hunter. I'm not the only one who agreed to work less…"

He kissed me on the forehead. "Off you get." He gently nudged me toward the door.

I should've argued, but those orgasms put me over the tired cliff and I still had work to do.

I dragged myself to my desk, packed everything up, and headed home. Once there, I grabbed the dinner out of the oven, went to my office, and opened my personal laptop. Time for job number two.

I just hoped all this work was going to be worth it. Tomorrow would be the moment of truth on if we'd wasted our time or not. Unfortunately, tomorrow would also be a deciding factor on my future involvement. If this took off as Bruce said it would, I'd have some hard decisions to make, because Hunter was right—I couldn't keep this up. I had two full-time jobs. I'd have to choose, and I wasn't sure that I was going to choose Hunter.

Chapter 2

———❦———

MY EYES WERE glued to the screen of my phone when Bert pulled up outside. I didn't have any sales numbers yet, but the game was live. People could download it, anywhere in the world.

But was anyone downloading it?

"Good morning," Bert said as I climbed into the passenger seat.

"Hey, Bert. Did you download the game?"

"Yep." He held up his phone for me to see. "Right there. I even played a couple levels—it's pretty fun."

"Thanks."

The car pulled away from the curb. "When will you know if it is doing well?"

I refreshed the app store and started scrolling through the ranking. "I think it takes a while. The marketing campaign starts today. Bruce seems to think the strategy is genius, but he's not a marketing guy. There's no telling if his plans will work. He probably plastered up a few flyers on the corkboard at his local college thinking that was still how college kids got their news."

"I thought he had a really profitable—get out of the way, you…" I grabbed the handle on the door as Bert swerved. "What is it with Mercedes drivers? They think they own the road."

"You are driving a Mercedes, Bert…"

"Exactly—why can't they drive like me?"

I didn't point out that they were.

Bert turned onto one of the busy streets that ran from one end of the city to the other. "Anyway, I thought the owner had a really profitable business before this?"

"Yes, but he had no idea how it exploded. He's really smart, but there's a reason he sold to Hunter."

"Oh. Well, I'm sure he knows a thing or two. But how is he paying for ads? On his own dime?"

"No, he got investors. He incorporated his business. I own a bit of it, as well as some investors. I mostly just look after the code, though."

"I still don't know how you do it, Livy. I really don't. Working for Mr. Carlisle, I wouldn't have the stamina to work for anyone else, and I mostly just sit around, waiting for someone to need a ride."

"I'm tightly wound."

He blew air out of his nostrils, his version of tsking. He pulled up in front of the office building. "Okay, Livy. Text me if you hear anything."

I thanked him for the ride and made my way in, gripping my phone the whole time. I dropped my bag on the floor and checked my phone again. No change.

Brenda came down the hall as I received a text.

Kimberly: *Good luck! I'm so excited!!!!*

"Why the constipated look?" Brenda asked as she set Hunter's coffee on my desk.

"You're a real gem, you know that?"

"Why yes I do." She sipped her coffee, looking at me over the rim of the mug. "Well?"

"My game went live."

"Oh, right." She went back and settled in her desk. She fished her phone out of her purse. "I was supposed to buy that."

"It's free. You just download it."

"Right. And how do you make any money?"

"Jesus. Does no one play games on their phone?"

Brenda swiped at the screen. "You need friends your own age."

"It's free to play for a certain number of tries, but then you can buy more lives, and various other components to enhance the game. You buy them all in the app."

"Ah. It's that kind of racket, is it? Okay—oh, here it is. That's a fun little picture. Oh crap...what's my password..."

I rolled my eyes and grabbed Hunter's coffee. I wasn't sure if her download was worth the aggravation.

HALFWAY THROUGH THE day I sat at my computer,

shoulders tense. There was a mountain of work to get through and I hadn't been able to focus on any of it. My phone lay on the desk right next to my keyboard, staring up at me.

I tried to resist.

Grunting in frustration, I swiped the screen and tapped into the app ranking. Bruce said we most likely wouldn't see anything for a couple of days as the game gained momentum, but I couldn't help myself. The dial spun, updating. I flicked my finger, watching the ranking upload as the numbers got bigger. I let out the breath I was holding as one hundred blazed by.

"Oh my God!" I jumped up. I snatched my phone and clutched it in both hands. "Yay! It's at one-thirty-five! That's something."

"Oh yeah?" Brenda got up to look. She wasn't in the habit of checking her own phone for anything. Her kids still called her work line.

I held the phone toward her and pointed.

"Cool. So you've got a few downloads."

"Yeah… I wonder how."

"How many friends you got?"

"Like…three."

Brenda scoffed and grabbed her coffee cup. "Let me refill before you head in to Hunter. I'd hate to have you make two trips."

"I get the feeling you aren't as excited as I am…" I scowled at her, but my smile came right back. I logged out and called Bruce.

"What's up?" he answered.

"Did you see? We're in the ranking! On the first day!" My voice was so high I was squealing.

"Oh yeah?" Why did Bruce and Brenda sound exactly the same? "Looks like our marketing push is working. I figured it would."

I shook my head and blinked. "You need to be more excited."

"It's only day one, Olivia. As my kid would say, 'slow your roll.' We don't want to be a flash in the pan. We want longevity."

"You sound like Hunter."

"I take that as a compliment. Okay, gotta go. I have a list of things I still have to do, including take my wife to dinner."

"Okay, well, I'll keep—" I brought the phone away from my ear, realizing that the call had been disconnected. "He *acts* like Hunter, too."

"How?" Brenda put Hunter's coffee on my desk and then sipped her own.

"He stopped saying bye when he hangs up." I grabbed the mug and headed into Hunter's office with barely contained excitement. Bruce might not be fazed, but this was my first business venture. I was over the moon that it was at the tail end of the ranking. I'd take flash in the pan over mildly sizzling into a fast death.

As I closed the distance to Hunter, my heart was racing and my smile was plastered over my face. I took in his handsome face, then connected with his sexy, smoldering stare. "Guess what?"

His eyes started to twinkle as I set his cup in the corner of his desk. "What?"

"The game—" A horrible pinch in my abdomen assaulted me. It felt like a hard, fast cramp. I reached for the edge of his desk, knocking the coffee forward and spilling some of the contents. I didn't notice. Pain radiated through my lower half, a more pronounced cramp now.

"Ow…" I put my hand to my lower abdomen.

"What's happening?" Hunter was up immediately. He came around the desk and bent over me, his hand gentle on my back. "What's the matter?"

I took a deep breath. Ordinarily this wouldn't be a big deal. I had cramps every month, often more violent than this. But I shouldn't be having cramps now. I didn't think I should, anyway.

Another wave of pain radiated through me. Was the baby in trouble?

Fear pulsed. Tears came to my eyes.

"Something might be wrong," I said in a quivering voice.

Hunter didn't say another word. Neither did he panic, like I was about to. In a quick movement, he scooped me up into his arms. We were walking toward the door a second later, his powerful strides taking us from the room.

"Mrs. Jones, get a car out front. I'm taking Olivia home."

"Yes, sir. Is she okay?"

Hunter didn't answer. He held me like a fragile vase, completely cool. He might've been waiting for the elevator on any normal day.

I put my head against his neck as another cramp vibrated through me.

"Try to relax," Hunter said softly as he entered the elevator. His voice was a tranquil breeze. "You've been very stressed lately, and along with excitement and today's events, your body is probably reacting. You just need to calm down. Take deep breaths."

I did as he said, but as another burst of pain made me whimper, I couldn't ease away from the fear that something was wrong. That I might be miscarrying.

"Deep breaths, baby. It's going to be okay." Arms not even quivering from holding my weight all this time, Hunter walked out through the lobby like a man on a mission. If there was anyone better in an emergency, I hadn't met them.

The car waited outside, its flashing lights signaling that it planned to double-park for as long as was necessary. Bert rushed forward when he saw us. "What happened? Do you need help?"

"Everything is fine, Mr. Ramous." Hunter stopped next to the car with a white-faced and concerned Bert looking over his shoulder. "Are you bleeding, Livy? Can you tell? I need to know if we should go home, or to the hospital."

"I don't know," I said, my hands shaking.

Hunter looked at me for a moment before bending to sit me into the car. "Take us to the emergency room at California Pacific, Mr. Ramous."

A moment later Hunter sat in beside me and took my hand. His eyes were deep and comforting. "It's going to be okay, Livy." His voice took on that commanding edge, filled with power. "You need to relax."

I took a deep breath, closing my eyes and leaning toward him. He pulled me in tighter. His strength and solidity wrapped around me, stilling the tremors. I trusted in his voice. In his presence. "Okay."

Hunter took out his phone. After tapping the face a few times, he lifted it to his ear. "Yes, Dr. Cheung? Hello. I have an emergency. Are you on duty?"

Hunter had set me up with Dr. Cheung as soon as we heard I was pregnant. The man knew someone important in every profession.

We pulled up outside the hospital a half-hour later, navigating through the San Francisco traffic as quickly as possible. "Should I wait, Mr. Carlisle?" Bert asked as he hustled to get my door open.

"Yes. I'll text you if anything changes."

"Yes, sir."

Hunter helped me from the car and then scooped me up again.

"I can walk, Hunter," I said as he began his purposeful stride.

"And I could just stand by and watch you go through a scary experience from a distance. I'd rather be doing something." He stalked toward a waiting room next to a store selling flowers and teddy bears. He set me down gently.

"I'll go to the restroom," I said. "Just to check on what's happening."

Hunter was pulling out his phone again. "I'll be right here if you need me."

I made my way across the lobby, savoring his confidence that everything would be fine. Once in the restroom, with hands still shaking, I locked myself into a stall and pulled up my skirt to assess the damage. My eyes filled with tears as I saw a bright spot of red. "Oh no."

I did my business and lined my panties with toilet paper. I wasn't bleeding that much, but I was still bleeding. I didn't know what that meant.

I walked slowly back to Hunter, trying not to break down. When his gaze found me, I saw a glimmer of fear spark in his eyes, but then the power and confidence returned. He was completely in control.

"The doctor is on her way. She's getting everything set up." He ushered me toward a chair. "Are you still cramping?"

I let my hand drift to my stomach. "No. But I'm bleeding a little—" I cut off as a sob choked me. "Hunter, I'm scared."

"I know. It's okay. It's going to be okay." His arm tightened around me. "This is going to be fine, Olivia. Just take it easy. Breathe deeply."

I nodded and burrowed into him as much as I could, desperately trying not to panic. It had only been two months, but I'd already fallen in love with my baby. I wanted to meet him or her, and then watch as Hunter held our child for the first time.

"Here we go." Hunter helped me stand.

"Hello, Livy. Mr. Carlisle." A short woman with crow's-feet at the corners of her eyes and deeply etched laugh lines around her mouth walked up with hurried, purposeful strides. Her gaze fell on me and a supportive smile took over her face. "Please, come with me." She turned and gestured us on, no doubt thinking we'd both walk beside her. She didn't balk, however, when Hunter swooped me up again and easily kept pace.

"Why don't you tell me what's wrong?" Dr. Cheung said as she directed us to the elevator.

"I had some cramping and now I'm bleeding a little." With her prompting, I told her how bad the cramps were and the color of the blood.

"Uh huh." She took us through a few halls and into a room with a bed covered in white paper. "Just sit her on the bed. And you are the father, Mr. Carlisle, correct?"

Hunter hesitated. His glance came to me for a brief second. "Yes..."

I wished I hadn't heard the question in his voice. This was a terrible time for his past to get in the way.

"Yes," I said firmly. Despite my fear and panic, I leveled him with a glare. He reached forward and took my hand. It was a wise move. I didn't want to have to break his kneecap for emotionally abandoning me at a time like this.

"And did you want him in the room for the examination?" she asked me in a slightly softer voice.

I knew what she was asking. Would I mind if he saw me spread my legs and show the world my hoo-ha. And frankly, as terrified as I was, I did a little. It had taken me years to feel comfortable presenting myself for an examination for a *doctor*. The man who used that area as a playground was another situation entirely.

"He's okay to stay if he wants to," I said in a little voice. If I was expecting him to man up, I had to do likewise.

"I'll stay," Hunter said, this time without hesitation.

"Okay." The doctor put her hand on the dreaded stirrups. "Why don't you go ahead and use the restroom. I'll need a urine sample." She handed me a small cup. "When you get back, I'll need you to undress. Just the lower half. Here's a drape." She put the drape on the edge of the bed.

I ducked out of the room, shadowed by Hunter. He didn't seem to want to let me out of his sight. That was okay by me. Except for the bathroom. I shut the door right in his face.

After I was done, which turned out to be a meager amount since I'd gone earlier, I handed over the cup and then took off my skirt and undies. Hunter helped me tuck the drape around my hips before I settled back on the bed. I didn't bother telling him I'd have to pull it out from under my butt in a moment. This was awkward enough.

After I was settled, the doctor wheeled a metal tray full of instruments toward me. "And how severe was the cramping?"

"At first it was like a bad pinch, and then like period cramps."

"Uh huh. And the bleeding sounds like it was fairly light. Okay." She motioned me forward.

With a sideways glance at Hunter, I scootched up into the incredibly awkward position where she would examine me.

"Knees, please." She touched my knee, indicating I was supposed to relax and let them fall to the side naturally.

There was nothing natural about this position in front of my boyfriend.

Dr. Cheung felt my abdomen and then examined me. After a moment she said, "Your cervix is fine. I don't see any cause for alarm at first glance, but it is somewhat fragile. Yes, there—just a touch, and there's a little blood. You'll have a little more bleeding from this examination, but don't let it cause you any alarm. Okay."

She pulled back her instruments and gave my knee a quick pat before turning away. I took my legs down, adjusted the cover, and scooted back. She opened a folder and started jotting things down. "It's pretty normal for women to have some spotting in the first twelve weeks of pregnancy. This is often caused from extra blood flow to the cervix, in which any contact with the cervix can cause some of this bleeding, like you saw. This can also be caused from stress, lifting heavy things, or fatigue. It's best to avoid those, and whenever possible, lie down and relax if you feel your body reacting.

"The cramping is probably also a sign that you've been too active, or putting your body through too much. If you ever feel a tightening, definitely slow down. Sit or lie, drink some cool water… It's good to keep an eye on it, so to speak. Give me or one of the nurses a call if you're concerned. As it's subsided now, I'm not too worried. I would caution you, though, to take it a little easier."

I got the stern look doctors were known for, and a matching "I told you so" look from Hunter.

"I want to have an ultrasound, just in case," the doctor went on, tidying everything. "If everything looks good, I think you'll be fine until your next checkup as long as nothing else happens."

I took a big breath and let it out. Relief washed through my body. "Okay."

"All right. Go ahead and get dressed and meet me out at the nurses' station when you're ready. I'll walk you down." She smiled at me, then nodded at Hunter.

When she'd gone, I moved to get off the bed. Hunter pulled me up and hugged me close to him. "Everything is fine."

That was Hunter-speak for "what a huge relief!"

I hugged him tightly before I disengaged so I could get dressed. "I panicked a little."

"That's okay. It's scary. It's a little life we're trying to protect."

I pulled on my skirt and let him help put me to rights. This was his version of taking an active role. I loved it. It was the Hunter I always craved. The one he still hid from strangers behind his distanced, unfeeling business mask. The guy he no longer hid from me.

"One last test." I smiled when I felt his hand on the small of my back, directing me through the door and to the doctor.

"All set?" The doctor smiled at me again and led the way. She didn't comment on the fact that Hunter let me walk this time. The fear had mostly passed.

The next room was larger, with a big machine, screens, and room for a few people. There was only one woman in there, though, tapping something into a computer resting on the machine. She glanced up when we walked in.

"This is Dr. Lund," Dr. Cheung said as she stopped near the door. "She'll be performing the ultrasound. I'll leave you in her very capable hands. Just call me, anytime, if you're worried about anything else. Okay?"

"Hello, Mr. Carlisle," said Dr. Lund, a woman with frizzy blond hair. "Mrs. Carlisle, go ahead and put this on for me. Just disrobe from the bottom down."

"Oh, I'm not—"

"Here, Livy," Hunter said, his eyes soft. He handed

me the sheet.

I stared at him for a second as a thrill of warm tingles seeped through my body. He'd stopped me from correcting her!

Oh my God, did he want to marry me? Obviously he'd tied himself to me forever with the baby situation, but...*did he want to marry me?*

My thrill was short-lived. The stirrups came out a moment later. Apparently this test would be a bit more invasive than on the TV.

Glancing at Hunter, I went through the same rigmarole before settling onto the bed and waiting for the instruction to scoot my butt to the end and throw my knees in the air. It came as expected, leaving me in another precarious position.

"All right." Dr. Lund wheeled her chair closer to my knees while still on the side of the bed. She didn't plan to take up the normal gynecologist position, it seemed. She held up a thick plastic thing that looked like a wand. I knew exactly where that sucker was going.

I glanced at Hunter again. Now that the danger was largely gone, this was damned uncomfortable.

"There is some small risk in performing an ultrasound this way," Dr. Lund explained, lubing up the end of the wand. "However, Dr. Cheung has given the go-ahead. It looks like your cervix is fine to handle it, and you're young."

"Dr. Cheung expressed some concern about her cervix being fragile," Hunter said, stepping closer. He put his hand on my shin protectively.

I was clearly the only one thinking this situation was awkward.

"The exterior of the cervix, yes. The wall. That doesn't mean she has a *weak* cervix, however. Meaning it doesn't have any bearing on her ability to hold a baby in the uterus. Since the fetus isn't large enough for us to get a reading with the fetal Doppler, we'll need to get a reading this way. The assurance greatly outweighs the risk."

Hunter nodded and stepped away a little. That explanation passed muster.

I was glad he was pulling police duty. All I could focus on was that large probe and my spread legs. I was not having fun...

"Okay..." Dr. Lund let the word trail away as she directed the probe into a personal place. She put a hand on my knee as she looked at the scene, jockeying the wand into position. It jabbed me in a way that made me wince.

Hunter stepped forward again, eyes on me.

The doctor noticed. "It might be a little uncomfortable for a moment—I just need to find a good spot to hopefully..." I winced again before she paused. "There."

Before I could look over at the screen, I saw a look of pure wonder pass over Hunter's face. A smile lit up his features, turning him from merely handsome into the most gorgeous man I'd ever seen.

"That's our baby, Livy," he said, putting a hand on

my knee.

I followed his gaze. On the black-and-white screen was a tiny little blip clinging desperately to a wall in a cavernous location. The doctor hit a few keys on the keyboard and moved the wand around. I winced, uncomfortable. This time Hunter didn't notice. His hand was shaking on my leg as he watched the screen.

"Can you tell if it's a girl or boy?" he asked softly.

"Not yet. We won't be able to determine that until between sixteen and twenty weeks." Dr. Lund tapped another few buttons before moving the wand around again.

Hunter's gaze, dripping with both love and wonder, fell on me. He stroked my knee.

"It's yours," I said softly, wanting him to thoroughly connect with this moment. Not wanting his past to get in the way, as it so often did when he tried to open up. "That's your little baby in there."

He rubbed my knee a little harder before looking back at the screen. "Is the baby healthy? Can you tell?" he asked.

"It looks good so far." Dr. Lund hit another couple of keys before pulling the wand free. "These are just the early stages, but the heartbeat looks fine. From what I can tell, the fetus is firmly attached to the uterus wall. I don't see any warning signs right now."

She tapped my knee before wheeling closer to her keyboard and started to type.

I wasted no time putting down my legs and securing

the drape more firmly around my hips. "Can I get dressed?"

"Yes, go ahead. I'll send these results to Dr. Cheung. Is she your OB-GYN?"

"Yes," Hunter answered. He looked at me. "She's the best OB-GYN in the city."

"Yes, she's very good," Dr. Lund said, working at the machine.

That was fine by me. I'd had to pick a new doctor when signing up for insurance. I wasn't attached to the lady I had randomly picked out of a book, nor her nurse who had seen me a month ago to confirm I was pregnant and then ushered me quickly from the shabby room.

"Okay." Dr. Lund gave us a tight smile. "You'll probably need that pad. You'll have some light spotting from this, I'd imagine. It's nothing to worry about. Congratulations." She nodded at Hunter and left the room.

"Not great with the bedside manner," I mumbled as I practically dove into my clothes.

"This isn't something a doctor generally does, I don't think. This is more a nurse's duty. I requested a doctor to see you, though." Hunter rubbed my back. "Thanks. For that moment."

I knew he was talking about calling out that he was the dad. "We all have our issues."

"I don't have issues, Olivia. I have past…"

"Issues. That's what we, politely, call baggage. Or do you prefer I just call a spade a spade and say baggage?"

"Transgressions."

I laughed. I sighed hugely, letting the relief mask the niggling fear that something like this could happen again. I thought back to that little blip. *Our* little blip.

"We're having a baby," I said with a smile. "And it's tiny."

Hunter threaded his fingers into mine. "Yes. We are."

We walked out to the street where Bert was waiting with stress lining his face. "Are you okay?"

I leaned into Hunter. "I'm good. Everything is fine. I just have to take it easy."

Relief washed over his face. "Well that's a relief. Are you—" His gaze flicked to Hunter. He then snapped his mouth shut and turned toward the parking garage across the street. "I'll just run and get the car."

"I think the secret is out," I said as we waited.

"He doesn't know anything for sure. You can still keep it secret if you want."

"I kind of want to tell everyone, but will just stop with him for now."

When Bert pulled up, Hunter escorted me into the car.

"Where to, sir?" Bert asked.

"My house," Hunter said. "We need to drop Olivia off."

"I have a ton of work still to do, Hunter," I said. I felt the stress creeping back into me. I leaned against the seat and let my head fall to the side, watching the buildings pass. "You're probably right. But I do still have lots to do."

"I've been giving you things that aren't strictly necessary," Hunter said. "You're doing more than any of the admins before you. I need to make some changes." I saw Hunter glance at Bert before directing his gaze out of the front again. "We'll talk about this later."

Irritation welled up in me, bringing back a little stress. I took another deep breath and stared out of the window. When did I start getting so worked up about everything? It seemed like I redlined pretty easily. That was not great for the baby.

"This is going to take some getting used to," I muttered to myself.

A SHORT WHILE later, Hunter opened the front door and turned to me. I plainly saw regret in his eyes. "I do have to go back. I can't stay here with you."

"I know."

He paused, almost like he expected me to beg.

Would begging work?

I opened my mouth to apply a little pressure, but I knew that wouldn't solve the problem. Instead, I said, "How are we going to fix this, Hunter? You're in an extremely high-pressure job. You can give some of my work away, but that just means you have to stay longer. That's not going to work. Not in the long run."

He trailed his fingertips down my cheek. "I'll figure something out, Olivia. I promised I would be a good father. I will keep that promise. I just need some time. You're my life, now. My future. I didn't know happiness before you, and I couldn't have happiness without you. I'll protect you and that baby with everything in my power, but some things can't happen in a day. I need you to bear with me, okay? Like you promised."

I blinked away a tear. "Backing me into a corner with super-sweet words. I see how you roll."

I closed my eyes as he planted a kiss on my lips. Then the kiss deepened. His hands came around me, pulling me into his hard body. He stepped forward. My back bumped against the wall. My core blistered with heat. My sexy systems swelled.

"I need you, Hunter." The scare returned, having me hesitating. "If only to kiss."

He scooped me up and carried me into the house. He gently set me down on the couch before sitting down beside me. "We can do this safely," he whispered as his hand drifted down between my thighs. He circled my nub as his mouth made a trail up my neck.

"Oh God," I said as my head fell back. His lips connected with mine, needy and insistent. His fingers picked up pace. Heat unfurled in my body, mixing with love. I clutched Hunter's shoulders, falling into his kiss. The world dropped away. All I knew was Hunter Carlisle and this moment.

I moaned as pleasure spiked. Everything in me wound up. So tight. So hot.

"Oh!" I burst, bliss filling up my body. I sighed

against his lips as I shook.

His kiss turned languid. His fingers on me slowed down, but didn't relent. "How do you feel? Do you want another?"

I smiled against his lips. "I think this is the opposite of stress. This is safe."

I undid the top button on his trousers and slid down his zipper. I reached into his boxers and captured his smooth manhood, hard and huge.

He moaned as I fell into the kiss again. Not able to help it, wishing I could feel him inside me, I started with a fast pace, my palm gliding over that velvety skin.

"Hmm," he said against my lips as his fingers matched my speed.

Desire pumped through me. I leaned on him more heavily, stroking faster. Kissing harder. His touch, firm and insistent, sent pulses of pleasure through me.

"Oh God," I murmured against his lips. I panted, stroking. Feeling the heat against my palm. "Almost..."

"I need something to catch—"

I didn't wait for him to finish that sentence. As my body ramped up for that final blast, I bent down and sucked him in.

"Oh—" He switched hands like a pro, reaching around my body and continuing to pleasure me.

"Come with me, baby," he commanded.

Without warning, an orgasm tore through me. My body jolted and shook as he quaked under me, releasing into my waiting mouth. I exulted in the pleasure even as

I felt him shake.

When we were done, I wiped my face on his suit jacket.

"Dirty move," he said with a chuckle as he pulled me tight to his body. "But under the circumstances, I won't complain."

"I'm surprised you didn't say 'low blow.' Get it?"

"Hilarious."

"You're only just realizing that?" I kissed his neck as he sat with his eyes closed, resting.

Too soon he rubbed my back, a signal he wanted me to move so he could get up. When I did, he stripped out of his jacket and inspected his pants. They'd need to be changed, no two ways about it.

"What time will you be home?" I asked.

"As soon as I can, but don't wait up." He looked at me seriously. "I will keep my promise, though, Olivia. Just give me some time. I'll reward your patience."

"Yes, my liege." I gave him a salute.

His brow furrowed before a lopsided grin took over his face. He shook his head a fraction before walking off toward the bedroom.

I hauled myself off the couch and headed to my office. As I closed myself in and sat at my computer, my mind turned to what I wouldn't be able to get done for Hunter. Another wave of stress rose up. Then the fear of what that stress meant.

I knew I had to choose; that was a certainty now. The problem was, even if I knew *which* job I'd pick, I'd have to give notice. It would take a couple weeks to get out completely.

With my body's reaction today so clear in my mind, I didn't know if I had a couple weeks.

Chapter 3

"GOODBYE, BABY. I love you."

I felt Hunter's lips on my forehead and his light touch across my stomach. I blinked as his presence moved away. It took me a second to wake up, but when I did I caught his shape leaving the bedroom in the early morning twilight.

On a normal day I'd smile and go back to sleep, but this wasn't a normal day.

I came wide awake and grabbed for my phone. After punching icons with my thumb, I scrolled through the ranking, looking for Bruce's and my game. We'd hit thirty-one last night before I'd gone to bed. Bruce had said it was gaining momentum faster than he'd expected, and predicted it would keep climbing. The marketing strategy was just getting going, apparently.

I passed the thirties with a frown. Maybe he was wrong.

My gaze scanned, then stuck to a nice graphic, scanned, stuck—I wasn't seeing our game. As the hundreds passed, my heart dropped. It had been a fast rise, but I'd thought the fall would've been more gradual.

A stab of fear pierced me. What if people hated it? What if they'd started playing it because it was free and the graphic and description were awesome, but realized it sucked and left horrible reviews? A bunch of bad reviews would sink that game. It would prevent other people from trying it. Even if we fixed the problems, assuming it wasn't the foundation, people would steer clear if the stars were low for the rating.

Biting my lip, feeling the squeeze in my chest for possibly hurt feelings, I searched for the game. When it came up, I almost wanted to cover my eyes instead of meeting my fate.

Taking a deep breath, I looked at the star rating. 4.5 with one hundred and three reviews.

"That's not so bad," I mumbled.

I tapped the game and flicked to the reviews. Five-star, five-star, five-star...one-star. I homed in. I couldn't help it. The only bad review in the whole list, and it was the only one I could see.

From: GmeLovr
This is th worst game ever!!!!!!! Terrible it suks u in then u hav to pay!! Rip off. Dont waste ur time!!!!!!

"A little heavy on the exclamation points, huh?" I mumbled.

I hunched over the phone. I scrolled through the five-stars, some reviews lengthy, some small, all praising how fun and addictive it was. Then my eyes stuck to the one-star again.

I dropped the phone into my lap, dwelling. Maybe the fact that the gamer had to pay to keep playing was a bad idea. Maybe we should have just used this game to get people to play our stuff, and make them pay for a continuation. That would prevent people from being angry and feeling cheated.

I blew out a breath and looked at the time. Six o'clock.

I glanced up at the door as I rubbed my stomach, trying to simmer down my stress level. Hunter had left early. Usually he went to the office at seven.

My mind drifted back to that one star.

Could that one review really unseat our placement?

I updated the ranking again, and then scrolled through, going slower this time. Twenties, thirties…fifties, sixties… "Why so fast?" I said with that same sinking feeling.

I dropped the phone and felt despondency settle over me. I blinked at the soft light of the windows to clear the moisture from my eyes. Bruce said we wouldn't be a sensation overnight. It would take time. We might even need to climb out of the abyss with our claws to get noticed. He'd said to keep the faith.

This was probably a good thing. It would buy me time to get my life balanced out. With yesterday's scare still hanging heavy over me, I needed to admit that this was probably the best situation for my baby.

I took a deep breath, trying to clear away the disappointment. Good thing or not, I still hated to fail.

I thought about Bruce. He'd been so smug and sure of himself at launch. And when I'd called him last night squealing like a thirteen-year-old, he'd taken it in stride. The man thought he couldn't lose. Worse, he'd sucked me up with his infallible confidence.

I lay back down, my phone in my hand, and checked our downloads on the website dashboard. As it populated, I found myself blinking rapidly for the second time.

I sat back up.

The numbers were for one day. Just one day in the Apple app store—launch day, at that. There was a lot of room for free play before anyone would be tempted to pay. Not only that, but they would potentially play the whole game, beginning to end, for free if they just waited for their lives to repopulate. Bruce didn't expect any sales right away.

We'd made $2000. For the day.

"Holy shit."

I checked it again, made sure it was just our company and just that one game. It was.

As ninety-nine cents a hit, that meant a lot of people were buying. Sure, there were a couple of bulk options, but mostly it was just that one small purchase.

"Holy shit."

I hit the green call button before I knew what I was doing.

"Olivia."

"Oh. Um. Hey, Bruce. Sorry—I shouldn't be calling this early."

"No, it's fine. I'm just in the office now. What's up?"

He was talking about his home office, the place his wife was starting to hate. "I thought you were supposed to be a family man now…"

"The wife is working out and kids are asleep. I'm being sneaky."

I laughed, then shifted, getting down to business. "Did you see the bad review?"

"Which one?"

A zing of fear worked through me. I didn't want to have to face another. "I just saw one."

"There's one for the US store and one for the UK. They're pissed they have to pay for extra play. These types of games always get this kind of review. It won't affect us. On the whole, our feedback is extremely positive. We're doing better than I expected, and I was expecting miracles with the strategy we set up."

We? All I'd done was blink stupidly while he tried to explain our release schedule for the next couple of years. Hunter was teaching me the ropes of business, and I was grudgingly learning, but I was more partial to shutting off my brain and programming. I'd hoped Bruce's job would allow me to do that.

"I mean, the sales are great. I didn't expect that. I know we have a bunch of expenses to pay for, but still…that's a good haul, right?"

"Are you kidding? It's a great haul for the first day." I

could hear the excitement in Bruce's voice. Finally! "We were liberal with lives and playtime. More liberal than the other hot games in this category. This says to me that the players are so addicted, they are flying through. Yes, this is great news. Our testers loved it, but sometimes that means only the techies will get the game. This says to me that the average Joe gets it, too. We have a hit, girlie, and we haven't even released on the other platforms! This is just the beginning. You wait."

I felt a smile bud. Then wither. "But we've already fallen off the ranking. Don't we need to be on there longer for visibility?"

"What do you mean we've fallen off?"

"I just looked. I didn't see us."

"Wipe the sleep out of your eyes. We're number five."

Ah! Tingles worked through my body. I jabbed the phone, turning on speaker before going back to the ranking. Sure enough, right on page one, there we were.

Number five!

"I didn't really pay attention to the first couple. Holy crap, Bruce! That's insanely good, right?"

"It's beating our expectations, yes. We weren't scheduled to hit this high for another day or so. This is more word of mouth and reviews than it is our marketing efforts, I think. Very good news. Very good. I'm excited about this, Livy. We have the dream team. Now. What are you thinking for the add-on levels? Did you get my email?"

I stared at our game with a smile. Number five! That was so awesome.

What Bruce had said filtered into my excitement. Reality seeped in slowly as the time to officially get up approached. "I didn't. I had a medical issue yesterday so I didn't get as much done as I wanted to."

"Oh. Is everything okay, if you don't mind me asking?"

I blurted it out. "I'm pregnant. It's still early—I haven't hit that three-month mark, so don't tell anybody—but I had a bit of a scare yesterday. All the stress isn't good for me right now. I just have to figure out how to balance everything."

Bruce was silent for a moment. When he came back on, his tone was grave. "You should talk to Hunter about this. Remember my telling you that family was more important than a life of work? That includes this job, Olivia. You need to stay healthy. Tell Hunter what you have on your plate and see if he can organize things a bit better. I assume he knows about the pregnancy..."

"Obviously, yes."

"Keep your hat on, I was just checking. As a father, I can tell you he is probably hellbent on trying to build an empire. That's the second thing that went through my mind when I heard Mandy was pregnant. Right after the joy was terror that I wouldn't be able to provide for the family."

"I doubt Hunter is worried about money..."

"I had a nice little nest egg, too. Men think about

pregnancy differently then women. Women have the home-court advantage in this. To us, it's an abstract concept. We can see the effects of it, and we know it's ours in theory, but it isn't totally *real* until we can hold it in our hands. You feel it in your body—we just have to trust you that it isn't gas."

I snorted laughter. "Nice."

I heard chuckling through the phone. "What I'm saying is women get ready by nesting, and men like me prepare by setting up its future. That's all I knew to do. I wouldn't be surprised if that's what is on Hunter's mind too. Anyway, congratulations. Hunter must be over the moon. A few things make much more sense, now."

"Like what?"

"Nothing. Tell him about all this, though. About your workload. I know he wants you to succeed, and there is no one more OCD about business matters than he is. He'll figure something out. Hopefully that will be making you choose…"

"Don't start that again."

Bruce laughed. "All right. Well, when you can, take a look at that email. We're ahead of schedule, but I bet we'll keep moving toward number one. I'd like to be ready when the tidal wave of popularity comes."

I snorted. "You have a problem with confidence, anyone ever tell you that?"

"Like I said, the dream team. The game is sound, thanks to me, the play is addictive, thanks to you, and our business strategy is ingenious. Watch out, Angry

Birds, we're coming for you!"

I laughed in elation. "Okay, I'll call you squealing again if we hit number one."

"Look forward to your call."

I paused a minute, didn't hear his farewell, and said, "Okay, well…"

I still didn't hear it. I pulled the phone away and saw that he'd disconnected. "Good*bye*." Rolling my eyes, I got up to get ready for the day. I couldn't wait to tell Hunter.

AS NINE O'CLOCK rolled around, I strolled toward my desk, trying desperately not to dwell on all the work I had to do. I needed to keep the stress down. As I dropped my handbag and set up my computer, Brenda came toward me with Hunter's cup of coffee.

"Good morning. Everything okay?" She didn't set the cup on my desk like normal.

I gave her a relieved smile. "Yes. I'm good. Just a scare."

"Let me take this in to him and I'll hear all about it. You scared the life out of me!"

I waved her away as I stood. "I'm fine, really. You don't need to treat me like an invalid."

"I wasn't. Hunter said I should do the coffee duty from now on."

I stuck out my hand. "He's being absurd."

She didn't offer the cup. "Maybe, but he was being incredibly stern about it. Ridiculous or not, I'm not in the habit of crossing him when he's in one of those moods. It's not worth the hassle."

I shook my offered hand at her. "Give it. I'll take the wrath, the big ninny."

Her look was wary as she passed it over. "This better not stick me in the middle of anything. Oh, hey— speaking of being caught in the middle. Hunter's mom sent something here addressed to you." She pointed to the corner of a white envelope sticking out from a blank notepad. "It came in after you guys left yesterday."

"Are you hiding it?"

"Yeah. If she sent it here it means she wanted to by-pass Hunter, right?"

Curious, I set down the coffee. That was a good point.

I fished out the envelope and found an invitation to her house dated for two weeks' time. In it was a little note:

Dear Olivia,

I apologize for the late notice, but I didn't receive an acknowledgment from Hunter. I worried you two didn't receive the invite sent to your residence. Hopefully this one will find its way. Hope to see you.

Best,
Trisha

"She's addressed it to just you, did you notice that?" Brenda hovered over the desk. "She thinks Hunter deliberately didn't tell you about the dinner. He did that with Blaire all the time, so she had to invite Blaire separately."

I looked up at Brenda as those words sank in. "Why would she want Blaire there, firstly, and why would Hunter be trying to keep it from me? He already told her about us. She was over the moon."

Brenda gave a tiny shrug. More of a shoulder jerk, actually. She glanced at my stomach so fast it almost didn't register. She covered it by walking toward her desk. "He's a queer one where family is concerned."

Since when did Brenda lose the opportunity to speculate when drama was involved? That last comment had seemed a little dour, too. "What do you know?"

She tapped the spacebar on her computer to bring up the picture. "That's common knowledge. He has a colorful past, what with the maid and his dad and all that. Maybe he just wants to contain the potential crazy until he's sure."

I shook my head, mystified. "You know, don't you?"

"That you're pregnant? Yep." She clicked her mouse in a nonchalant sort of way.

"How could you possibly know? We haven't told anyone!"

Brenda gave me a leveling look. "I have been working for that man for years, Olivia. *Years.* You don't make the cut by being blind and rational. You have to learn his moods, fit pieces of a greater puzzle together—hell, you have to be a little crazy yourself. I know that man about as well as I know my husband. If he didn't pay so well, and throw so many perks at me, I would've quit a million times in the beginning. Trust me. I don't need the head-wreck."

"You're grumpy and insane, I get it. But how did you know?"

She shrugged, turned toward me, and sipped her coffee. "He flipped yesterday. I've never seen him react that way to something, and he's often in high-pressure situations. He treats you like a precious artifact usually, but even that has limits. Yesterday he left in a state of panic, and he came back relieved but overly determined. Something big is going on, and it's got him all riled up. I did the math."

"First of all, he didn't panic at all. He was the strong one. Secondly, you're full of crap. There's no way you pieced everything together from that and an invite. He told you, didn't he?"

She rolled her eyes. "He can hide things well, but you? When you don't feel good, you slump against the desk. You don't drink coffee anymore. You get hounded by Hunter if you don't eat—c'mon. I might not be Sherlock, but I'm no dunce. I already suspected, and his freak-out clinched it. I'm a little pissed that you barely got morning sickness, though. I threw up all day with both pregnancies. Just not fair. But then, my husband is the easygoing type. He didn't assume I would break at any moment."

"Yeah, well, he didn't have his dad steal his love and

47

his fake baby, either."

"True." Brenda's eyebrows rose. "How's he been? He believes it's his, I take it."

"Yes, but he has moments of doubt. He doesn't harp on it, but I can see the hesitation."

"He got screwed over. I don't blame him."

"What should I do about the invite, though? Why wouldn't he want to tell his mom? Because he *is* sure. We know for a fact that I'm pregnant, and he's admitted that he knows it's his." Hurt overcame me. "I don't like that he's treating this like he treated Blaire. That's not good."

Brenda drummed her fingers against the desk. "I know him well, but I don't know him *that* well, thank God."

"That's not helpful."

Brenda gave me a tight-lipped smile. "Ask him. See how that goes."

"Do I have the power to fire you?"

"This company had better hope not. I don't think you know how a calendar works."

I gave her a scowl, but she'd already turned back.

In trepidation, I walked into Hunter's office. He glanced up, looked at my face, my stomach, the coffee, and then my heels, in that order. He turned toward me and stood, coming forward to take the mug.

To his disapproving expression, I said, "Hunter, I'm pregnant, not an invalid. I feel totally fine. I'm very calm."

He steered me toward the chair in front of his desk

and sat me down. He returned to his seat with his coffee. "I don't want you walking in heels, Olivia. There's no point. You don't need to make things harder on yourself."

"I love you, but you're being ridiculous."

Power and authority infused his smoldering bedroom eyes. He leaned forward slightly, pinning me with his stare. "No heels."

The soft command sizzled down my spine and tingled my core. Facing the problem I always did with him, I lost the willpower to say no. "Okay."

His eyes softened, a result of winning the overprotective war. "How do you feel?"

I mentally checked in with my abdomen, as I'd been doing all evening yesterday and all morning. I half held my breath, terrified I'd feel another pinch, or worse, full-out cramp. All was calm, though. If I kept myself calm and balanced, everything seemed fine.

"I'm okay," I said in the face of Hunter's serious expression. What Brenda had said about him being wound up yesterday gave me a whole new light on the situation. He might not show it, but he was just as terrified as I was. Worse, he couldn't check in physically like I could. He had to sit in fear, and hope nothing went wrong, with only my occasional assurances. That had to be a tough position for a control freak like him. For *any* loving father, actually.

Regardless of the fact that it wasn't something I'd ever shared with a man, I completely opened up about my female stuff. "No fresh bleeding, no pain. The pad was clear. I feel okay."

He nodded and sat back, relaxing.

If only that was the only issue.

My mind went in two directions—one was the elation from my game, and the other was doubt over the invitation and what that might mean. I decided to explore the elation first. The other issue was squeezing my insides uncomfortably. "We're number five in the charts."

His eyes started to twinkle. He leaned back and threaded his fingers together in his lap. "I saw that. Great work. The response has been extremely positive."

My mind stuttered on his phrasing. Bruce had used nearly those exact words.

"Did you talk to Bruce?" I asked suspiciously. It was like him to check up on me. Not that I minded, but I liked to catch him when he thought he was using ninja stealth.

"I've been following along. It helps me anticipate your moods."

My stomach rolled. I was unable to push away the worry about him hiding me from his mother. Trying for an unaffected tone, I went for a logical lead-in, and mostly failed. "Speaking of moods, I got an invitation to a dinner your mom is having. She said she didn't hear from you…"

Hunter's look hardened. His broad shoulders tensed and his jaw clenched. He strapped on his business mask, his way of trying to distance himself from emotion. I was not making things easy on the poor guy.

"You used to do this kind of thing with Blaire," I said softly.

He didn't speak for a moment. Finally he said, "This isn't the same situation as with Blaire. Not even remotely. It's just..." His biceps flexed. He was uncomfortable and trying not to show it. Or maybe trying not to acknowledge it.

"You don't want to tell your mom in case it turns out that this baby isn't really yours, is that it? You don't want to look the fool twice..."

Pain and regret flashed through his eyes for a brief moment. "This is not a reflection on you, Olivia. I love you. I'm happier with you than I've ever been in my life. However, it's hard to confront certain issues."

Relief consumed me right before a surge of emotion welled up out of nowhere. I threaded my fingers together, trying to clamp down on the heat prickling the back of my eyes. I knew what he was going through. I understood why he wanted to close this off. I just wished my deeper desire to celebrate this new life would get in line with logic.

"Okay." I shrugged like it was no big deal. "It's your mom, so we'll do whatever you want. We can keep it a secret."

Like an avalanche, a wash of emotion ran over me. Fear, worry, the feeling of inadequacy and of being undervalued blazed. Worst of all, the fear of being abandoned while in a life-changing and precarious situation rampaged.

I was losing the plot! Holy crap, where did all this come from?

A tear leaked out. I brushed it away quickly, hating that I wasn't staying strong for him. That I was making this worse for him. My stupid hormones were going crazy!

"I'll just politely decline." I cleared my throat, trying to stop the quiver in my chin. "No problem. Okay, back to work."

"Livy—" Hunter got up and came around the desk as I was trying to make a getaway. He wrapped me into his strong arms. "I'm sorry. Truly. Like everything, I need to go at my own pace."

"I know." I curled up into his arms, feeling his possession of me. Giving myself into his keeping once again. "Tell that to my hormones."

He kissed the top of my head. "We'll give each other some room to act out of character, then."

"You might need to give me a *bit* more license in that regard, but yeah."

"I'm proud of you. For your game. I played a little—it's really addictive. You did a great job."

"Not really, if you only played a little…"

He backed up and lifted my chin with a finger. His lips slid along mine. "I love you." The kiss deepened, lifting my desire. His tongue danced in my mouth, light and teasing.

Expectation surged. Arousal raged through me.

I slid my hands down his hard chest and cupped his even harder bulge. "I emailed the doctor last night. We're okay for sex."

"There is no way I'm going to make love to you until we are absolutely sure, Olivia." He nibbled my bottom lip. "We'll talk about it tonight. Worst case, we can get to third base. Or is naked petting second base? I'm not clear on the bases."

"I haven't worried about bases since I was a virgin."

"So...a few months ago, right? Right before you met me?" I felt his lips turn up into a smile. "I never got that chance. I'm happy to have you be my first in that respect."

Warmth like I had never known unfurled in my chest. A love so profound that I didn't know how to handle it moved through me. It was like his statement had me connecting with that time in my life when everything was new and a little terrifying. When I explored, edging slowly into intimacy. He'd just opened that door for us, and the effect was just short of soul-wrenching.

A wash of tears drenched my face. Completely the opposite emotion, but exactly the same origin, I was out of control and riding a hormonal wave of crazy.

"Hey," Hunter said quietly, looking down at me with concern. "What happened?"

I smiled through my tears. "I'd like that. Being your first-base runner."

A small crease formed between his eyebrows. "These are happy tears?"

"Yes. Stop trying to understand. Just go with it. I am."

He smiled, making me blink up at his handsomeness. "I love you, Olivia. And I am trying. I'll make all this right. I'll be the man you need."

"Stop." I wiped at my face. "You're making the waterfall worse."

He kissed me again, full of love and longing, before backing off. "I have a lot of work to do. You're distracting me. I'll see you later when I can touch you."

My face heated, and then my body. I nodded without words and went out to my desk. It wasn't until later that I realized I was in the same boat, but for an entirely different reason. I didn't want to tell my mom, either. I knew she'd have her hand out almost immediately. Her pursuit of rich men would become the pursuit of her daughter's favor so she could sidle up next to Hunter and his fortune. He hadn't shrugged off marriage in the hospital, but he hadn't mentioned it, either. A part of me worried that if he was confronted with where I came from, he wouldn't be as open to my taking his last name. A bigger part of me wondered if he wanted to get married at all.

Chapter 4

———— ❦ ————

"WE DID IT! Oh my God, we did it!" I stood up from my desk with my phone clutched in my hand. I looked up at Brenda as she came down the hall with two cups for the afternoon coffee run. I pointed my screen toward her. "We hit number one!"

A cockeyed smile appeared on her face. She took her cup back to her desk, not commenting, leaned over her keyboard to type a few things, then turned toward me as her mug made its way to her mouth. That was it. That was her reaction—looking at me with a smirk while drinking coffee.

"Brenda, this is a big deal!"

"What happened?" Hunter came out of his office. I wasn't even annoyed that now he had Brenda message him so he could come out and get his own coffee to prevent me walking. My comment on that absurdity could wait.

I pointed the screen at him. "We're number one!"

He took a few steps, squinted at the screen, and then

straightened up with those delicious, twinkling eyes. "Great job."

"This is ridiculous. You two are killing my mood." I called Bruce, half bouncing in anticipation.

"Yallo?"

"Hey. We did it! We're number one!" I braced with my hands out, waiting for the reaction.

A couple of seconds later, probably the amount of time it took him to look it up on his own computer, he said, "O-kay. Excellent. Now we're in business!"

I smiled like a fool and took a deep breath. This was huge. Our first game. Our first time. There were so many apps and games, so many freebies, both big and small. We were nobodies with one game within the thousands, and we'd hit number one. I was so excited I didn't know what to do with myself.

"Now the real work begins," Bruce said.

I felt my smile wither. "You couldn't let me enjoy that a little longer?"

"We have to cash in on this momentum, Livy. To-night I'll run the update to limit how much we give away for free. I'll also check to see how fast people are getting through the levels. We might need to make them harder."

"The ones toward the end are difficult enough."

"There are some smart people out there with no lives. If all they do is play, we need to stay ahead of them."

I glanced at my computer, thought of the huge list of things I had to do for Hunter, and then the even longer list for the game. My whole body tightened up, immediately overwhelmed. I took a deep breath. I could do this. I could stay balanced and stress-free. "Okay, I'll—"

The phone left my hand. I glanced up as Hunter put it to his head. "Bruce, she has to go… Yup… Sure."

Hunted tapped it off and handed the phone back. His expression was not at all apologetic. "Send me your to-do list for both this position and for Bruce. That is top priority."

"Here we go…" Brenda murmured, setting her cup down and bracing her chin on her fist.

I felt my ire raise without warning. Frustration and anger turned into a lethal soup that zinged through my body. Then came fear of what those emotions might do to my baby. Finally came tears, because my hormones were so jacked up I didn't even know which way was up anymore. "Damn it, Hunter!" I yelled. I didn't know what else to do. He was right in taking the phone, and the stress, away from me, and we both knew it.

I hated admitting that, though. Yelling seemed like a better reaction.

Hunter's eyes lit on fire. "Come into my office."

"Please," I said through clenched teeth as I stomped after him.

As soon as we were both sitting, Hunter said, "You know very well that if I hadn't ended that call, you would've spiraled. I remember the same look on your face from yesterday, Livy, right before you bent over my desk holding your stomach. I've said before that my job is to protect you and that baby. If I have to save you from yourself, so be it. I make no excuses, no apologies. You need to choose, Olivia. No more delays."

Tears of frustration came to my eyes. "Look. If I don't do this stuff for Bruce, he'll replace me. I really don't want that, Hunter. I love doing that stuff."

Hunter's eyes softened. "So why don't you do it full-time?"

I scrubbed my palm against my knee. "What about you? You'd have to replace me."

"I can fill your role here much easier than Bruce can replace you should you quit. You need to do what you love, Olivia. We both know that administrative duties give you no satisfaction."

"But…" I looked around. My gaze snagged on the couch, and then slid by the desk. "What about the personal contract?"

"Is that what has you worried?" Hunter crossed his ankle over his knee. "And here I thought you were worried about me working more hours." A smile dusted his lips. "I have everything I need in you."

"Sometimes you forget, though. At least, when I started you did. You tried to call me in for a faceless screw, remember?"

His eyes lit on fire. I could read the desire in his look. "I don't look for mindless fulfillment now. I look for you."

The fear eased, but didn't totally disappear. "I don't know. If I didn't work here I'd never see you. There must be some way this can work."

"I'll see you every evening and you can visit me here. You can even come in and work at my table." He pointed to the round table in his office. "Or you can use the conference rooms. Or my couch. You shut everything out when you work and I find your presence comforting—I think that would be a great arrangement."

I bit my lip in indecision. This was all happening so fast.

In a last-ditch effort, leaning on my stubbornness, I said, "You can't force me to choose, Hunter."

"I can fire you. And I will. What you do after that would be your choice, but it also doesn't take a genius to know how relieved you'll be to work on your code without my duties nagging at you."

I frowned harder. "You sure think you know everything."

He grinned and pushed forward. "I do. Think it over."

I walked out of his office shaking my head. I hadn't stood a chance.

"Did you get reamed out or what?" Brenda asked as I sat at my desk.

"No. He offered to help me out by firing me."

"You two have a messed-up relationship, have I mentioned that?"

I snorted. "You didn't have to."

AT THE END of the day I left the office with a strange

sinking feeling. I didn't really want to quit working for Hunter. It was how I'd met him. It was how he'd more or less browbeaten me into loving him. Everything had started for us with my first yes in the park. I was reluctant to let that go.

Truth be told, I was also a little worried. I lived with him, and I was having this baby, but we hadn't talked about forever. The crazy-woman part of me didn't want to give him more space for fear he'd realize I wasn't nearly as great as he thought. I was a plain Jane next to him. Not forcing my presence on him every day might break whatever spell he was under. After that, kicking me out and arranging custody rules would be a cinch.

I needed to take my mind off this.

I took out my phone as I waited for the car service. It was seven o'clock. Hunter said he had another couple of hours to do before he'd meet me at home. While I should go home and work on the game, which was still number one, I wanted to chat with a friend. I wanted to take my mind off the big decision I had weighing on me.

I called Kimberly.

"Hi!" she said on the second ring. "You have ESP. I was just going to call you. How are you?"

I smiled at the peppiness in her voice. "Good. Want to meet for a coffee?"

"Definitely. I'm in the financial district. Where are you?"

"Same. I'm just leaving work."

"Dumb question, right?" She laughed. "Okay, I'll

make my way toward you."

The black car pulled up next to the curb. As the man got out, I took a couple steps toward him. "Sorry—false alarm. I won't need the car for a couple hours."

"Yes, ma'am." He didn't even look put out. For some reason, that made me feel guiltier about wasting his time.

Ten minutes later I caught sight of the shining red hair bouncing with each of Kimberly's steps. Her smile was bright and her hug warm when she reached me. "Hi!"

"Hey. Where to?"

"Jen and Rick are at a little café a few blocks from here. Want to go meet them? They're back together and fighting all the time." She rolled her eyes.

I hesitated. Jen and Rick would probably be drinking, as it was happy hour. Since I'd never refrained from drinking in their presence, they would immediately realize that something was up. I couldn't very well tell Kimberly no, though. Then she'd ask why.

Trying to cover up a pregnancy was not going to be easy.

"That sounds…fun," I said sarcastically.

She laughed and looped her arm around mine. "They usually cut it out when someone else shows up. What have you been up to? I saw that your app is at number one. How excited are you right now?"

"Super. Super excited! I should be working on it at the moment, but I just don't want to."

"How do you do it all? You're going to crash."

"I know. Hunter is making me choose."

She loudly sucked in a breath. "No! What did he say?"

I went over our meeting, what I was doing, and what it would amount to.

"And you're worried it'll be out of sight, out of mind, huh?" Kimberly surmised when I was done.

"It's crazy, I know."

"It is, but I totally get it. I'd think the same thing. Because, you know, you got the job because of the personal thing. He won't, though. The man is head over heels. Everyone talks about the smart girl who reeled in Hunter Carlisle. You're a legend."

"Smart girl, huh? Usually I'd be proud of that, but Hunter is so gorgeous. People should be talking about the pretty girl who reeled him in."

Kimberly scoffed and playfully hit my arm. "You're beautiful. But beauty is a dime a dozen. Hunter has always had beautiful girls around him. He chose the genius girl."

"*Genius?*" I laughed.

"Not like I'd set them straight." Kimberly stuck her tongue out at me before pulling my arm toward the door. "This is it."

She entered before me and hesitated in the entryway.

"Two?" a hostess asked, reaching for menus.

"No. We're here to meet—oh, there they are." Kimberly pointed at a table in the back surrounded by four people. She turned to me with wide eyes.

I groaned. Jonathan, my ex-boyfriend, was one of the four, along with Tera, who was a snob at the best of times.

"It's fine," Kimberly said as she pulled me toward the table. "He knows you've moved in with Hunter. You're out of his reach."

"It doesn't prevent him from trying to be buddy-buddy with me to get closer to Hunter. He'd push over his mother to get a job in Hunter's company."

"Hey! Olivia!" Rick stood up as we approached and brought me into a tight hug. "Long time no see."

"Hunter Carlisle works you too hard," Jen said with a smile, standing up to hug me too. She then organized the chairs so we could fit at the table.

Tera gave me a smug smile before firmly putting her hand high on Jonathan's thigh. "Hi, Olivia. Hey, Kimmie."

Kimberly's fingertips dug into my arm. She'd realized the same thing I just had. Tera was dating Jonathan. He'd dumped me because I wasn't good enough and here he was, letting Tera rub his upper thigh while she sent me gloating glances.

If she thought that I'd be jealous, she was delusional. "Hey, everyone."

"I heard you have a game out. How cool is that?" Jen beamed at me.

"Kimmie was really pushy about getting us to download it," Rick said. "Now I'm addicted." He gave me a comic frown. "Not cool!"

"What's this now?" Tera asked. Her hand ran over the swell of Jonathan's bulge. Her eyes twinkled as she looked at me.

I barely prevented myself from rolling my eyes. "I helped design a game. It's doing pretty good so far."

"Pretty good? That thing is rocking." Rick tapped his phone and then pointed the screen at Jonathan. Tera leaned close to him so she could see better, and to smear her body against his.

I didn't have to refrain from rolling my eyes that time—I just joined Kimmie and Jen as they did it.

The waitress stopped beside our table. She looked at Kimberly and then me. "Can I get you guys anything?"

"We need to celebrate," Kimberly said as she fingered the small menu. "Beer or shot?"

I tried not to groan. *Here we go.*

"I'll just have a Sprite," I said to the waitress. "My stomach isn't feeling the best. I might be getting sick."

"A Sprite? Nah. We're celebrating! Have a beer." Kimberly looked at the waitress. "We'll have beers."

"No, really—" I cut off as I felt a warm hand on my arm. I looked over at Jonathan, who was making Tera sit farther back so he could lean across her to touch me.

"Hey," he said with a warm smile. "You really designed that game?"

Confused at his touch and his tone, I stuttered out a "Yes."

Jonathan took his hand back but continued to lean against the table, his full focus on me. "That's pretty remarkable. And how about Hunter Carlisle? Do you still work for him?"

"Yes. For now."

"I can't believe you moved in with him," Jen said with stars in her eyes. "When Kimberly told me I flat-out refused to believe it. Hunter *Carlisle*! I didn't think he could be caught."

"Are you saying you'd dump me to get a piece of him?" Rick said with an annoyed expression.

"Does everything need to be about you?" Jen shot him a glower. "I'm trying to talk to Livy."

"What do you mean, for now?" Tera asked.

The waitress showed up with a round of beers and distributed them before asking if we wanted any food.

I leaned back, away from it. "That game is a lot of work," I told Tera. "I'll need to choose which company I work for."

"No-brainer," Jonathan said. "Hunter Carlisle."

"Well…" I shrugged. "That's just admin work. I'd really rather do coding."

Jonathan gave me a placating kind of smile then, in a condescending voice, said, "You get to learn business from a genius. I think that is worth the price of admission. He can open doors others can't. You'd be a simpleton to walk away from that."

"She *lives* with him," Kimberly said with spice in her voice. "She's not walking away from him; she's doing something she's obviously better at. She can still learn from him."

"Dude, you're full of shit." Rick waved Jonathan away as he took a swig of his beer. "You have no idea what you're talking about."

"Here, Livy." Kimberly moved my beer closer to me as she picked up hers.

"No, I'm okay." I lightly touched the bottle, nudging it away a little.

"You're really not drinking?" she asked, hesitating with her own bottle.

Most people hated peer pressure. Kimberly thrived on it.

"Why aren't you drinking?" Tera squinted at me.

The table fell into silence, all eyes on me.

"I have to work after this," I hastened to say. "Beer makes me drowsy."

"You still have to work?" Rick said. Tera was still staring at me, suspicion in her eyes. Her gaze dipped to my stomach.

Suddenly, I knew exactly what she was thinking. I'd trapped Hunter with a baby. He was the unattainable bachelor. No one had ever been able to land him. Except for me, a girl without money and without awe-inspiring beauty. And suddenly I was pregnant.

It did look bad.

"Excuse me," I said as I stood. Tera squinted again as she looked at my belly.

In a strange sort of panic, I made my way to the bathroom. This was silly. Who cared what people thought? I knew that Hunter loved me. I'd known it before the baby. In fact, he'd been the cause of this. He was the one who'd tried to get me without protection as often as possible. I certainly hadn't trapped him.

But man, it sure did look like I had.

I washed up and analyzed myself in the mirror. I had a tiny paunch. Not at all noticeable. Most people would assume it was chub. I took a deep breath and made my way back out. I was all sorts of off balance with life. I needed to get a grip!

"Livy."

I started and then stumbled into Jonathan. He caught me by the shoulders and directed me toward the wall so people could get by. "Careful," he said with a smile.

"What's up?" I asked, taking a step away. He was standing much too close.

"Hey, you know, we don't talk anymore. I miss that."

"Yeah, well, you broke up with me. It kind of put a damper on our nonexistent friendship."

He chuckled and placed his hand on my shoulder. "We were friends. I had a great time with you. We should hang out sometime."

"Um…" I was sure my smile screamed out my discomfort. I dipped and shifted like some weird dance, hoping to dislodge that hand. "Maybe."

"Yeah. You know, I have some great ideas that Hunter Carlisle might be keen to hear. I mean, I have a job, but I'd entertain making a change if the money was right."

"A job, right." I dipped again before stepping away. His hand slid off. "You'd probably be better off seeing what openings there are in the company. I don't think there is much right now."

"Well, that's what I wanted to talk to you about. Or him, if you thought to bring him around. I could—"

"Olivia." The power and command in that tone had a delicious shiver dripping down my back. I looked up as Hunter came to stand beside me. His arm worked around my waist before pulling me in possessively against his side. His sexy, smoldering eyes trained on me for a moment before swinging to Jonathan. He didn't utter a word, but the question was obvious. What was my ex-boyfriend talking to me about in the back of the restaurant, away from everyone else?

This also looked bad.

"Hello, sir." Jonathan smiled, oblivious to the aggression radiating from the man beside me. "I was just mentioning to Livy that we should get together for a chat."

"I told you to stay away from her," Hunter said in a low tone.

I looked up at him in surprise. *When?*

"Yes, sir, I realize that. I wasn't thinking to meet her alone. I'd hoped you—"

"C'mon, Olivia. We're leaving." Hunter firmly directed me in front of him. With his hand on the small of my back, he guided me toward the table so I could get my handbag.

"Is that your beer?" Hunter asked in what I could only describe as an extremely dangerous tone.

Oops. That looked even worse.

I had been chatting with the ex-boyfriend in a secluded spot with a beer waiting for me at the table. I was not batting a thousand on this little trip out.

"I didn't drink out of it," I said in a rush.

"Hi, Hunter," Jen said, standing and throwing out her hand to shake.

"Hey, man." Rick stood, too, but his smile was hard. He kept glancing at Jen, who was doing a poor job of hiding the lust sparking in her eyes.

"Do you need a ride, Kimberly?" Hunter's hard gaze hit her.

She glanced at her beer as her face turned bright red. She snatched her handbag off the chair and stood, making no move to drain the last of her beer. It looked like she thought she was in trouble for drinking because I was.

"Okay," she said in a demure tone.

Without another word, Hunter directed me out of the café and to the car waiting by the curb. He had been as rude as usual, but I didn't dare call it out. I was in so much trouble it wasn't funny. Going along quietly until I could assess the damage was the name of the game.

Chapter 5

"OKAY, LIVY, I'LL talk to you tomorrow." Kimberly gave me a wave and a grimace as her gaze touched on Hunter. I think she knew I was in trouble even though she didn't know why.

When the car was on its way again, Hunter said, "What were you doing with him?"

"He wants a job. He's seeing Tera now."

"He's fucking Tera. He won't take her to meet his parents."

"That's...some personal knowledge. How do you know that?"

Hunter looked at me, anger and suspicion in his eyes. "He broke it off with you because you were from a lower social class. He loved you, Olivia. The slander he spread after he broke it off was hollow. Now that you've been elevated to a higher class, he'd be more than happy to get any part of you he could."

"How do you know all this? And when did you tell him to stay away from me?"

"When I realized he'd be a possible threat, I made sure that I remained informed. I didn't like hearing that you were with him this evening, after assuring me you were going home."

"I didn't *assure* you. And I didn't know he'd be there."

We arrived in front of the house. Hunter's mouth was a thin line as he helped me out then guided me up the front walk. Once inside, he turned to face me. His muscles flexed and relaxed, his temper burning hot.

"You told me you were going home," Hunter said in a flat tone.

"And then I decided to meet up with Kimberly. She said Jen and Rick were at a café, so we met them. I did not know he'd be there, Hunter, seriously."

Hunter turned toward the stairs without another word. He'd go dunk himself in work and try to put some distance between himself and this situation.

I trudged into the kitchen with a surly attitude and found Janelle at the stove. She looked up as I entered. "Hey. I'd thought you'd be home earlier, so I'm just heating up your dinner. Was that Hunter I heard?"

"Yes. He's home."

"Oh, okay. I'll just make a plate up for him."

She busied herself as I sat at the table in the corner. "I wish I could have a glass of wine right now." I'd told the house staff about the pregnancy for meal preparation and various other things.

"If wishes were unicorns we'd all have a ride to

work."

I leaned against the tabletop. That wasn't helpful.

"What's up?" Janelle asked as she got out the milk. "Why the long face?"

"Hunter caught me in the vicinity of an ex-boyfriend. Now he's mad."

Janelle gave me a grimace and then a puzzled expression. "Hunter doesn't seem like the jealous type to me."

"He had a weird past and this baby is bringing it all out again. He's not really rational."

"Oh, right—I heard something about that. This has got to be tough on both of you, then."

"Yes. For a lot of reasons. There are a lot of changes."

"There always is with a baby."

That also didn't help. She was too practical by half. I wanted someone to allow me to mope and wallow.

After I had eaten, I headed toward my office. I needed to make Hunter talk about things, but I also knew he was shutting down like a clam. I was exhausted, stressed, and unsure. I didn't think I could work up enough anger to barge in there and demand he get over his issues.

Instead, I worked until my eyes drooped, which was not long at all, then slunk into my room. I was asleep soon after my head hit the pillow. We certainly wouldn't be running bases together that night.

THE NEXT MORNING I took the coffee from Brenda. The uncertainty from the night before had grown into a tsunami of doubt. Hunter had come in last night, showered as normal, and then turned his back to me when he got into bed. He'd never done that before. Never!

He hadn't kissed me goodbye that morning, either, or said he loved me.

I made my way into his office silently. Filtered light from an overcast sky softly touched his shoulders and made a halo of light around his handsome face. My heart clenched as I neared, hoping I was making too big of a deal about all this. Hoping I was being a stupid girl.

He didn't look up. I might've been a ghost with an invisible coffee cup. It was like in the beginning of my employment when he had kept me at an arm's distance.

Choking on my fear, I stood for a moment, looking down on him. I wanted to open the lines of communication and sort this out, but I didn't know how to start. His jaw was clenched and shoulders tensed. I could tell that he just wanted me to go away.

I set the cup down gently, still staring at him. His fingers moved over the keyboard, typing out an email. He didn't intend to acknowledge my presence.

Downtrodden and miserable, I made my way back to my desk.

"What's your problem?" Brenda asked. "Do you feel like crap? Because that would make me feel less jealous of your easy pregnancy so far."

I set up my computer, and then spilled. "Hunter kinda found me at a café last night standing close to an ex-boyfriend. It was totally innocent, and not my idea, but he went a little…"

"Crazy?" Brenda turned toward me and picked up her coffee. "Then what happened?"

"Well…he also saw that I had a beer. I wasn't drinking it—they ordered it for me. But it looked all kinds of wrong."

"I'll say. That certainly didn't help. Then what happened?"

"You love this drama, don't you."

"Yes. New love is like a soap opera. So?" Brenda's brow lifted.

"He's super distant now. He won't even look at me. I don't know what to do."

"Uh huh. Hmm. What would not-insecure Olivia do?"

I frowned at her. "I don't know that version of Olivia. Does she exist?"

Brenda smirked. "What would the Olivia that balked on signing a contract do? Surely she wouldn't take this lying down…"

I thought back to that time, when the stakes were nothing more than not giving myself for free. That had seemed like a serious issue at the time. Now I had a baby to think about, not to mention a place to live, a job, a future…

"Uh oh—you're going haywire." Brenda got up and grabbed a bottled water from her drawer. She handed it over. "Drink that. You need to calm down. I don't want to get in trouble for making you panic. Mr. Overprotective would probably fire me."

"I wasn't too thrilled about the overprotective issue until I landed in this place, where he's really distant. Now I want that other guy back."

"You'll figure it out. It's up to you, though. You've always been the one to steer him where you needed him to be. Left to his own devices, he would still be in his ivory tower, shut away from the world."

Brenda went back to her computer.

"That's it? Just dump a 'you'll figure it out' and turn around?"

"Yes, Chicken Little. That man thinks the sun shines out of your ass. He's going to grapple with this until you drag him out. Bet you."

I scowled and tapped my phone with a heavy finger. The ranking was as I had left it, Bruce's and my game on top, garnering downloads and making a small pile of money.

Why was it when one part of my life was going well, another part fell to pieces? It was one of life's cruel jokes.

I clicked into my email, saw a bunch of things I needed to work on, and zoned out for a moment. I didn't really want to set up a meeting schedule for the rollout of some new software I didn't know anything about. It was mind-numbing work. The alternative, though, was learning about something or other that I had no interest in. It wasn't business in general, it was how this company operated. I really didn't care.

I glanced longingly back at my phone. I could be

writing code for the new levels. I had a dynamite idea that would bend people's brain in the right ways. I just knew it. I wanted to get to it.

Hunter's words came floating back to me. Choosing.

If I chose what I loved to do, I wouldn't have access to Hunter all day. He'd said I could work from his office, but if he didn't want to see me, that offer could easily be revoked. If we had a fight, like now, I'd sit at home thinking about him, hoping he didn't lose his head and screw the secretary.

"I'm in a fix, Brenda. I really am." I leaned my face against my fist in a pout.

"Fix a sandwich. Hey—" She turned to me in a sudden gush of impatience. "Get that schedule done. I need to fit Hunter into it somewhere."

"Pushy," I muttered, reaching for my mouse.

THE DAY PASSED with me acting like the coward I was. I'd been into Hunter's office a few times, delivering coffee or papers. Instead of talking to him, as Brenda kept urging me to do, or wrecking his head, like I was accustomed to doing, I just stared like a window shopper. It must've been really weird from his end of things, but he never turned toward me. Never said a word. He was really putting his all into ignoring me.

At six o'clock I tapped my phone, checked my ranking, and then the reviews. I skimmed passed the first horrible one, then the next. I'd seen those already. My eyes glazed with all the five-stars. Some people really did like the game.

My gaze snagged on a new one-star review.

"Stop hating the game!" I seethed at the phone. Then I groaned. I had been waiting for a review like this. It was a long, drawn-out affair from an educated person who could string a couple words together. Proper grammar and no typos made this person's critique so much more valid.

I read the person's opinion in trepidation. Apparently, my game was trite and unoriginal. The graphics were pleasing but play was clunky. It wasn't hard in the least and it price-gouged. This person thought that the designers were beginners, and it showed.

My heart sank. This person had exposed the weaknesses perfectly. We *were* beginners, for the most part. And there *were* some clunky places. Trite, unoriginal? Yeah, I could see that.

I hunched in my chair. Something snapped. I could only be the victim for so long.

"I can't have this many critics in life!" I stood in determination.

"There you go! Give him hell!" Brenda put her fist into the air as she put her glasses into her handbag.

I marched into Hunter's office, pushing aside my fear of what would happen if this conversation went badly. If he lost his marbles and pushed me away, I'd lose the love of my life, sure, but I wouldn't be destitute. Bruce was still paying me, the game was increasing in momentum instead of decreasing, and I could stay with Kimberly until I found another place to live. I could even move somewhere cheaper. Working for Bruce meant my laptop was my office. He lived in Middle America where rent was a quarter the price of San Francisco. I could easily move near him.

Strapping on my big-girl panties, I came to a stop right in front of Hunter's desk. Face schooled into a bulldog-looking expression, I stared down at him with my hands on my hips.

He ignored me.

I'd heard of people *staring harder*. I had to admit, however, that I didn't know what that meant. Should I lean forward with the bulldog expression? Was that what would do the trick?

Couldn't hurt.

I added a lean to the situation.

Now I was just staring closer with what was probably a constipated expression, I had no doubt. If he didn't look up at this, he was being obtuse on purpose.

"I'm not posing for a wax sculpture, Hunter. Look at me."

His hands stilled over the computer. His arms flexed. Slowly, he turned his head in my direction. His power and command blasted through me, turning my spine to Jell-O and setting nervous tingles through my body. His hard eyes and clenched jaw made me want to back up and apologize for bothering him. He was firmly in his business pants, cast away from the world on his secluded island. This was the Hunter Carlisle the world saw. The one that hadn't opened up to me. That hadn't kissed me.

"What do you think is going to happen, Hunter?" I said, standing tall despite my desire to roll over and play dead. "Do you think I'm going to leave you for Jonathan, or something?"

He didn't speak. Just stared at me. If this was a video game, my skin would probably melt off from his laser vision.

"Even if I did, Hunter, it would still be your baby. This isn't like with your dad. That baby wasn't yours. It was a lie. This isn't. I'm pregnant with your kid, and if you pull out, and leave me, I'll be trying to raise this little beast on my own. And I don't know that I can do that. I'm scared, too, Hunter. I'm scared of how this will change my life. I'm scared of giving birth. And I'm scared that something will go wrong and I'll lose something that I've grown to love so, so much."

I wiped at my face. I hadn't expected to break down. I'd planned to yell, if need be. Not whimper. I couldn't help it, though. What I had said was true. I *was* scared. I needed him. I wouldn't lose anything by letting him know it.

"I need you to be a man, Hunter. I need you to be *my* man, and not go running at the first small issue we come across. Because there will be many more things that remind you of your past. I'm sure of it. Are you going to fly off the handle for all of those?"

I tried to regain my hard stare. Instead, I had soggy eyes and a trembling lip. So much for the tough-girl approach.

Hunter sagged a fraction. He lowered his eyes to his desk. With a small shake of his head, he stood slowly and came around the desk. When he reached me, without a word, he pulled me into his hard chest. "This isn't easy for me to let go of," he said in clipped tones. "I am swinging between wanting to walk away from you to save myself eventual pain, and locking you up so I don't have to worry about someone else getting you. I realize both of those things are ridiculous, but do you see how an innocent encounter morphs into a disaster? All I hear is that I'm not the father. That it was all a lie."

"It's yours, Hunter. I'll repeat it as often as I have to. Seriously, Jonathan was just trying to get a job. He wanted to meet us both to chat. It's you he's after. I need to be jealous of him running off with you, not the other way around."

I felt a tiny squeeze. "I wanted to kill him. Still do. Stay away from him, Olivia. I can't be rational where this is concerned. There's too much at stake."

"I was already trying to stay away from him. Kimberly didn't know he'd be there. She didn't know he was with Tera, either. The whole thing was weird, actually. But you have nothing to worry about."

"And the beer?"

"I tried to order a Sprite. I was distracted by Jonathan wanting to tell you some ideas he thought you'd be into. Before you jump at it, he has a job. He'd be willing to hear your offer, though. Just so you know."

I felt another squeeze. "I'll have to go with you to these meetups. Make sure they know not to pressure you."

I thrilled at the idea. "You don't need to be overprotective, but hanging out with my friends might be nice. Having a life isn't just a young man's game, Hunter."

"I need to try harder, is that what you're saying?"

No, it wasn't. But if that was what he took from it, I wasn't going to say boo!

"I'll arrange it," Hunter said softly.

"You don't have to arrange a meetup. You need to loosen up. I'll just call Kimberly and see what she's up to next time you take an hour away from work. No biggie."

"I saw that your game is still on top. Congratulations."

Ah. The ol' diversion technique. He was going to arrange it anyway.

I decided not to push. One thing at a time. "Yes. I saw the latest terrible review before I came in here. It's a doozy."

"You shouldn't look at reviews. It won't help you."

"Some might. The critical ones."

"You'll dwell. It won't do you any good. There isn't a single game in the charts with that high of a rating. What you designed is working. When did you plan to develop new levels?"

I leaned my forehead against Hunter's chest. "I'll start working on it tonight."

I expected Hunter to remind me about my forthcoming decision, but he just stood and held me silently. It was louder than if he'd uttered the words.

I ran my hand up his chest and angled my face to him. His came down immediately, connecting his lips with mine. I fell into the kiss, into the solid warmth around me, his firm touch. My body heated up.

Before I knew what I was doing, I had his jacket halfway off.

"Are you sure?" he asked with a heady voice.

I hadn't seen any more evidence of danger, and the doctor had given me the go-ahead shortly after I was discharged. It was a green light.

I ran my hand over his bulge, deliciously hard. It was all the answer I needed.

He scooped me up and carried me to the couch. Once there, he set me down on my feet and kissed down my neck before sliding his lips over my collarbone. Air caressed my skin as he worked my blouse open. Then his hands felt up the outside of my thighs.

I worked his buttons down, opening his shirt to reveal smooth skin. His glorious pecs and cut abs greeted me. I kissed down his chest as I undid his pants. Reaching in, I captured his smooth shaft.

He moaned softly. I stroked as I ran my tongue around first one of his nipples, then the other. I ran my palm over his pec again. His chest might've been cut from stone; it was so perfect while being intoxicatingly warm.

I straightened up to capture his lips. I lifted my skirt

so his manhood could reach between my thighs, rubbing just right.

"We need to go easy, okay, baby?" Hunter murmured, lowering himself to sit on the couch.

"Not *that* easy," I responded, straddling him. I gyrated my hips forward, reaching behind me and through my legs, capturing his hard cock against my lace-covered core. I kissed him harder, needing him. Loving him with everything I had and wanting to show it.

Without preamble, I pulled my panties to the side and angled up. His tip slid across my wetness. I moaned, directing it to my opening, and then sat down.

"Hmm, Livy," Hunter said against my lips. "I love you."

I ran my fingers through his hair as I let my head fall back, savoring the feeling of him filling me up. I moved my hips in a slow circle, enjoying the friction. Feeling the intimacy with Hunter, I rose before lowering again, straight down, taking him deeply into me. I moaned as my body tightened up.

I pushed his head back so I had better access to his lips. I took him deep before backing off. Deep again, then back, loving the feeling of him inside me. I nibbled his lips as cracks started to work through me, the pleasure coursing, eroding my control. The kisses became more fervent. I invaded his mouth with my tongue as I moved up and down.

"Oh," I sighed, the desire rushing now. My movements became rougher. I sat and pulled back up, tightening up. Needing him. Needing to finish.

"Yes, Hunter," I exulted, closing my eyes and tugging on his hair. I crashed into him now, everything condensing. My body on fire. His lips on mine. "Oh, yes. Just a bit—"

I squeezed my eyes shut as the pleasure turned white hot. I panted, my heart beating faster, love filling me up. The sensations unfurled and took me higher. Blanking out my mind. All I knew was him and pleasure.

"Almost… Almost…" I strove harder, him inside of me, the friction exquisite. The couch squealed as it rocked against the floor.

I blasted apart, everything exploding into pleasure so intense it fused my jaw shut. Every muscle flexed over him. I shook with my release as he tensed in climax under me, the orgasm so intense I couldn't even cry out.

I slumped forward. Another wave of pleasure washed over me, making me tremble. Finally, I started to relax in the glow of one awesome fucking orgasm.

"Holy crap." I gave another little tremor as I melted around him.

"We should fight more often. Makeup sex really is everything it's made out to be."

I laughed softly and threw my arms around him. "I love you, Hunter."

He kissed me softly and sat idly for a moment. I knew his mind had probably already turned to work, but he was giving me a second in the afterglow. It was quite a difference from the first time we were together.

"How do you feel?" Hunter asked after a few minutes of quiet. "Any cramping or signs of danger?"

"I feel good. No discomfort. No pain."

"Good." He kissed my temple and I knew he'd reached his limit.

I got up with a grin. "You made it five minutes that time. That has to be a record."

His scowl wasn't the response I was looking for. "I'm not in the habit of taking my time when the door is unlocked during working hours. I can make it up to you tonight..."

"Ha!" My blurted laugh made him scowl harder. "I wasn't commenting on your sexual prowess." I laughed a little harder as he helped me put my clothes back on. "I meant afterward. You hung out longer instead of running back to your desk."

"Oh." His expression cleared. A twinkle infused his eyes but he didn't say anything else. Instead, he finished straightening up before he finally made his way to his computer.

Even the great Hunter Carlisle, Sex God Extraordinaire, got twinges of performance anxiety. Who would've thought?

Still chuckling, I made my way back to my desk. Before I reached the door, though, Hunter said, "I'll see you at home."

I stopped with my hand on the door. "Huh?"

He looked up from his desk. "Your day officially ends at six o'clock, like Brenda. I want you to leave at the end of the day. No exceptions."

"But I still have—"

"No exceptions," he repeated in that commanding tone. He turned back to his computer. That was that.

He was employing the ol' *force Olivia's hand* technique. Sneaky.

And I knew, sooner rather than later, it would be effective.

I put everything away and made my way home. It was time to put the big-girl panties on for a second time, and do the scary thing. I was about to choose my future.

Chapter 6

———❦———

I WAS SITTING with the letter on my desk as Brenda walked up with the mug of coffee. She put the white porcelain in front of me and stared, as she basically did every morning these days. My life was her largest source of entertainment.

"You need a life," I said.

"I have a life. A boring one. What's the look for?"

"Nothing." I looked at that stark white envelope. "Just going out on a limb."

"Did you get a visit from Ed McMahon?"

"Who?" I checked my ranking. The game was still on top of the charts, puffing out its feathers with pride.

"I hate it when you make me feel old." Brenda walked to her desk. "What's on the day's agenda?"

I took a deep breath, picked up the envelope, and stood. "You won't like today's agenda much. I'll let it be a surprise."

I ignored her rumpled brow as I made my way into Hunter's office. Friday was a good day to quit.

I put the mug down in its place. I laid the envelope a little further in. Then I turned and got out of there like the coward I was. Back at my desk, I stood with a stiff back, opening and closing my hands to expel some nervous energy. I couldn't believe I was doing this. This was a huge risk. I might lose my new job. Hunter might find a secretary he wanted to date instead of me. The sky might fall. All terrifying thoughts.

I sat and stared at my computer. I kind of hoped he looked at the resignation letter right away. This was a loaded situation.

"Wait…should I have told him in person that I was resigning?" I had asked my computer, but Brenda didn't know that.

"You *what*?" She swiveled toward me. "Get back in there and burn that envelope. You can't resign!"

I grimaced at her. She scowled back.

"What are you going to do instead?" Her gaze hit my phone. "Oh, poo. You're going to do that game thing, aren't you? Damn it. You like that better. Are you getting paid? You don't want to just keep doing it on the side? No, you probably can't, can you. Hunter won't let you go gray this early in life. Well, shoot. This puts me in a pickle."

"Are you talking to me or yourself right now?"

She shook her head at me. "Selfish."

"Wanting to be happy is selfish?"

"When it makes me have to work harder, yes. You should sacrifice for me." She leaned against her desk. The grumpiness didn't clear from her face. "Are you excited or is Hunter making you quit?"

"He is making me choose. I'm sure he's not going to dump me if I don't work here, so I figured I'd do the thing I liked better. He said I could work in his office, though. I can visit."

Her eyebrows arched. "I wouldn't if I were you. He'll hire someone that's not as smart as you, and then you'll just have to help her do a mere fraction of your job. You should stay away until the new hire finds her feet."

"Uh huh. Back to the original question, should I've told him in person? I probably should've."

"Couldn't you have told him at home? Why so professional all of a sudden? But yes, you should've had a meeting and told him in person before you handed in the letter."

"Oh." I stood, a ball of nerves all of a sudden. I peeked into his office. I could just make out his broad shoulders still turned toward the glare of his computer. I walked in gingerly. I could probably snatch the letter back and do a meeting, but he knew it was coming. It'd be best if I just tossed it out there. When you were screwing your boss, professionalism wasn't the order of the day.

As I neared the desk, though, I saw the letter open, pushed off to the side. It rested on the open envelope.

I paused.

He glanced up, and then sat back, clasping his hands in his lap. Neither of us spoke.

I cleared my throat. Then pointed vaguely toward his desk. "You, ah…read the letter, then."

"Yes. I've put in for a temporary employee. Or will, I should say. I'm proud of you. I think you made the right choice."

I straightened up a little. That was nice to hear. "You're not mad that I'm leaving you in the lurch?"

"Not at all. I expected this. I'll start interviews right away. As soon as I can get someone reasonable, you can train him or her, and then leave. Most of your job isn't something a regular admin can do. You've been doing tasks above your pay grade."

"And above my intelligence level, I know."

His eyes twinkled but he said nothing.

He wasn't supposed to agree with me.

"Are you calling me dumb?" I said, cocking my hip to the right.

"You were able to do every task I set you. If they were above your intelligence level, you wouldn't have been able to. Modesty just wastes time."

"You could do with a little modesty, actually," I muttered.

A smile curved his lips. "Are you confident with this decision?"

I shook my hand, palm up then down. "So-so. Bruce is bankrolling my salary right now. This might not pan out."

"Investors are bankrolling your salary."

"Still. It might not pan out. Then what will I do for

money? This is kind of a big risk. I never would've done this if you hadn't pushed me to it."

"Money is not a concern of yours, Olivia. I'll guarantee income. You need to focus on your happiness."

My heart warmed. I leaned against the chair facing his desk. "That's nice. It doesn't really apply, but it's nice."

"Why doesn't it apply?"

I hesitated. To me it was pretty obvious. If the worst happened, I needed to look after myself. We weren't married—his money wasn't mine. I made my own way in life. If Hunter did a one-eighty, I'd need something to fall back on, and my savings right now weren't big enough.

I couldn't say any of that, though. He wouldn't understand, and because of that, I'd sound like I was hinting for a proposal. I'd already triggered enough of his hang-ups—a week of smooth sailing would be nice before I pushed something like *that* on him.

"I just want to do well at this game," I said to deflect.

He looked at me for a while in silence, his expression blank. I had no idea what he was thinking. Finally, he said, "Did you need anything else?"

"No. I was just making sure you got the letter. Brenda said I should've had a meeting…"

"I pressured you into this. A meeting might have been overkill." He turned back to his computer.

"Wow. Mr. Charming today, huh?" I turned and made my way back to my computer. I was pretty sure normal resignations didn't go like that. Still, it was done.

THE WEEKS WENT by relatively quickly. While I was supposed to leave work at six, Hunter didn't enforce quitting time once I'd decided to leave the company. Instead, he had me help with finding my replacement. To the surprise and confusion of his peers, he chose an older woman with a husband and kids. It was the first time in years Hunter hadn't hired a beautiful, young assistant. Brenda said there was a lot of gossip, but since no one said anything directly to me, I ignored it.

I trained the new assistant as best I could. He'd been right, though. The stuff she had to do was basically fielding questions. Instead of tweaking budgets or creating marketing timelines, she was instructed to send those tasks to the respective VPs to be handled in-department. The result would be a much slower turna-round, but less actual work for that admin.

Once I'd finished training my replacement, and stopped working for Hunter, it was just me and my laptop. I could get up whenever I wanted. I could wear yoga pants and a holey shirt all day if I felt like it. To do actual work, I could stay in the house, go to the beach, or whatever. The world was my oyster.

I'd never been so lonely during the workday. I'd also never missed Hunter more. I even missed Brenda's surly attitude or Bert driving me into work. I loved my new job, but I missed having coworkers to talk to.

And now here I was, two months after I'd quit, making my way to the place I chose to work more often than not.

"Livy, let me get that!" Bert hurried around the car toward me. He took my computer from my shoulder and then took me by the arm, escorting me to the car.

Bert had not recovered from my scare. He thought I was breakable, and once I'd started to show, the man was worse than Hunter.

"It's not heavy, Bert," I protested as he led me to the passenger seat. He opened the door before handing me in, then stowed my computer in the backseat.

"How are you today, Livy?"

"I'm okay. I have to go up a size in clothes." I bit my lip to stop my smile. I had a baby bump! I still half couldn't believe it.

"My wife used to love Gap. They're expensive, though."

"I think Hunter told Janelle to get a bunch of stuff. He doesn't trust me to get the best."

Bert smiled. "I should've known, yeah. At least you don't have to worry about it."

"Exactly. I wasn't complaining."

"How's he doing? He's working long hours, huh?"

I looked out the window. Yes, he was. Very long. He left the house at six most days and didn't get back until ten or eleven. He came home a smidgeon earlier on Sunday, but otherwise, he worked seven days a week.

"Have you ever seen him look so tired?" I asked.

"Sometimes, if he's got something stressful going on,

but…"

I nodded, because I knew what he was going to say. Hunter had stress and tired lines under his eyes and lining his face. This pace was taking its toll. For a man that had made work his whole life, it said something that what he was putting himself through now was wearing him out.

"I just don't understand," I said to Bert. "What is he doing that takes this many hours?"

"Have you asked?"

"Yes. He just says to give him time. That's it. He needs time to get everything organized. The man can plan out a whole chess game after my first move, so I know he's got something figured out, but… I don't know. I'm worried and feel responsible at the same time."

"He's getting everything ready for you and the baby. I remember working a lot of hours when my wife was expecting our first. I was trying to get enough for a house. I did it, too."

"I know. Bruce said something similar. But Hunter has a house. A few houses. And cars. And a bunch of crap he doesn't need."

"I don't know, Livy. I've never understood him. Ask Brenda."

"I have. She's really tight-lipped about it. She knows something, but that woman is a vault. It's annoying."

A laugh died in the back of Bert's throat as we pulled up to the building. Before I could say anything, he was out of the car and hurrying to my side. He grabbed my computer and helped me out of the car.

"Seriously, Bert, I can manage. Wait until I get really big before you hem and haw."

"Okay, Livy." He held the door open before following me in.

I held out my hand for my computer. Just like yesterday, and the day before, and every day since I'd decided to spend my time coding here, he ignored my hand and followed behind me.

Yes, this was the definition of crazy—doing the same thing and expecting different results. But I really hoped that someday he'd catch on.

I rolled my eyes as he waited right behind me for the elevator. Then followed me in.

"You need to get a little dog," Brenda said as I came into sight. She looked over her half-moon glasses at me. "Usually the big bodyguards are carrying the celebrity's dog."

"He followed me in again. I had no choice."

"I know. But you need to get a dog. Do you not listen?"

I stopped in front of her desk. "What's got you so bitter?"

"I'm always bitter."

"Your scowl is more pronounced than normal. What's up?"

"I don't see a difference," Bert said behind me.

I stifled a laugh as Brenda intensified her scowl at

him. "That one"—she jerked her head to the currently empty desk beside her—"can't keep up. Neither could the one before her. Hunter is working them all to death."

"You, too?"

She sniffed. "I know the end game. I can hang in there."

"What end game?"

Her lips pursed. She looked back at her computer, pulling a Hunter. She planned to ignore me now.

I rolled my eyes. They had plans, and they weren't telling me what they were.

I walked into Hunter's office, prepared for my favorite view of the morning. I got exactly what I was expecting. The light streaming over Hunter's broad shoulders before I feasted my eyes on the most gorgeous man I'd ever seen.

I smiled, reveling in his splendor. "Hey, baby."

Bert unslung my computer on the table. "Okay, Livy. Call me if you want lunch." He nodded at Hunter. "Mr. Carlisle."

Hunter rose from his desk and came around, his eyes soft and a small smile dusting his face. "Good morning. How are you?" He wrapped an arm around my back and put his palm on my baby bump. "And how's the little one?"

"Good. Both good. I'm worried about you, though. This is starting to get out of hand, Hunter."

He kissed my lips softly. "God, I love you so much, Livy." He rubbed my belly. "Don't worry about me. Let me worry about you. How was the ride in?" He directed me to the chair at the table.

"Same as always." I took the proffered seat.

"Do you need some water or tea?"

"No, that's okay. I can get it. Carey isn't my assistant, she's yours."

An edge crept into his voice, his business tone and power infusing his words. "You're a guest and she gets paid to distribute beverages to guests."

Guest? I was practically a tenant. "I'm good, Hunter. I'll get it when I need a break."

After a moment he kissed the crown of my head. "Get to work, then."

Fawning one minute and commanding the next. The man had issues.

"Hey, did you see this?" Brenda popped her head in the office and held out an iPad.

"Brenda, you can just tell me where to look on my phone. You don't need to bring in your iPad every time you see my game…" I laughed as she walked closer, holding out the screen for me to inspect.

"My kids pull this stuff up. I don't know how to find it. Look—" She pointed to the familiar graphic of Bruce's and my game. Apple had given us a banner on the storefront.

I couldn't wipe the smile from my face. It was just one of the many awesome things that had happened with the game in the last two months. It had taken off. Flat-out gone wild. Our game had stayed number one for a solid month. That was almost unheard of. It also hit number one with the Android market, on PC, and even did well on e-readers that could download apps. Money was pouring in. Enthusiastic fans clamored for more levels, more! We'd created a hit.

Thank God I'd switched jobs when I had, because even working full-time, I was hard-pressed to stay ahead of the players. I was trying to get the next game going, too, working through the same process with that. I never had an idle moment, and I loved every minute of it.

Soon after the game blew up, I thought Bruce was going to have a meltdown. After all, wasn't this a replica of his first company? It grew into a sensation virtually overnight and blindsided him with demands?

Amazingly…history didn't repeat itself. It was like he was expecting it. When we needed programming help, he was already on it. When we got a mention on the *Ellen DeGeneres Show*, Bruce was ready with a marketing boost directly after. The man was on fire! He'd definitely learned how to run a business. And he still gave his wife plenty of face time. Win-win for him.

"Yeah, they are pushing the game again because we got a mention on some comedy show," I said. "They called us 'wonderfully addictive.'"

"Huh." Brenda looked at Hunter, who was watching us. "I thought it was boring. I just don't get all these electronic games. I'd rather just read a book. My kids finally played, though. They liked it. Have you played it?"

"I have, yes." Hunter's eyes sparkled as he looked at me. "I'm waiting for harder levels."

I sniffed. "You're a little smarter than our test demographic, Mr. Snobby."

Hunter had ripped through the game in record time with very high scores. I was currently developing a game just for him. I'd stump that bastard if it was the last thing I did.

With that, I fell into my coding. The more I kept his focus, the longer he'd have to stay tonight. I wanted some fondling time. I hadn't been able to stop at third base yet. He got me so worked up I strived for home every time.

Tonight, though, I'd show him what he had missed when he was a teen. I fully expected him to hate me for it.

Chapter 7

"HEY, BABY—" HUNTER stopped in the doorway.

"Do you need to shower?" I asked innocently. I was lying on the bed in his pajama bottoms and a tank top that didn't completely fit. It stretched along my baby bump, showing clearly that I was expecting.

His head shook slowly as his eyes traveled my body. His tie was loosened and his button-up shirt was open down the front, revealing an undershirt hugging his cut pecs and lying against his flat stomach. He unthreaded his tie all the way and pulled it from under his collar. He walked to the end of the bed before shrugging out of his shirt and then pulling off his undershirt.

I sucked in a breath at the most exquisitely cut chest in the world. The thing was bumpy and delicious. I got why women salivated just at hearing his name.

Seriously, how the hell did I get so lucky?

He stripped out of his pants and crawled onto the bed in his boxers, already tenting.

"You look beautiful," he said as he stretched out beside me. His hand traced up my hip and in, over my stomach and up. He didn't touch a breast. Instead, he skipped over and ran his fingertips lightly along my chin. He leaned in, grazing his lips across mine.

Shooting sparks of expectation lit me up. I ran my hand up one powerful arm and then down his side, feeling the play of muscles as he, in turn, ran his hand back down my side. I felt him deepening the kiss before leaning, gently pushing me to my back. He didn't lie on me, though. Instead, he traced my stomach with his hand again, lightly. Softly.

"When are we going to tell your mother?" he murmured against my lips.

I tensed, not expecting that question. It needed to be done, I knew. She was my mom. For better or worse, I really should tell her big news like this.

"Soon. Probably. I don't know. Maybe next month."

"Why not this weekend?"

A surge of panic had me pushing him away without realizing it. He lifted a little, looking down at me with those bedroom eyes, reminding me of sexy nights.

I turned my head to the side. "She'll just be weird about it. She already calls me periodically to ask how it's going with you. With this she'll probably turn up at your doorstep with an overnight bag."

"*Our* doorstep. And what is your concern? That she'll ask for money?"

I rested my hand on Hunter's big shoulder. "Truthfully...I'm sure she will. I don't know if she pissed away all her money, or she's just afraid it'll run out because she's never really worked and won't start now, but that's why she's always chasing rich men. She's after their money. She thinks I'm giving her an 'in' with you. This would be a big, golden gateway as far as she's concerned. You don't want to be subjected to that."

"I wouldn't be. I'm no stranger to people wanting my money. What would make it easier on you, though?"

I laughed sardonically. "I have no idea."

I felt Hunter's fingers apply pressure to my cheek. I let him pull my face toward him before he planted a sweet kiss on my lips. "Let me run interference. I can handle your mother."

"You don't know my mother. She can wear down a rock."

His lips connected more soundly. "I'm more head-strong than a rock," he mumbled against my lips.

"Certainly denser. I can't argue there." I smiled as I ran my hand down his smooth back. "Why do you want to tell my mother when you are ignoring yours like the plague?"

Hunter kissed me soundly, stealing my focus. His issue with his mother was completely forgotten for the moment. He was definitely great at running interference.

He opened my mouth with his, then explored with his tongue. His hands found my breast now, kneading. His finger traced around my nipple, making me moan.

"Wait, wait," I said, already out of breath. My sex pounded, begging for him. But this was a return to the past. I needed to stay in the safe zone, whatever the hell that was.

The irony of being knocked up out of wedlock, and then trying to pretend I was a virgin, was not lost on me.

"Go slow," I said against his mouth. "I don't want to have sex."

His body peeled away from mine in a flash. His hands were gone the next second. Cold air replaced his heat, and made me shiver.

"I didn't mean I *can't* have sex, just that I don't want it," I clarified.

"Why? What's wrong?" I heard the panic lining his words.

Perhaps I should've approached this a little different-ly...

"I'm fine. And can have sex. And want to have sex. But I think it'd be better for you if you... Look, I'm trying to stop at third base, okay?"

He blinked at me for a second, as if trying to process the crazy words coming out of my mouth.

"This just got awkward," I muttered. I grabbed his thick arm and pulled. "C'mere."

A confused grin lit up his handsome features. "Do you think you can hold out?"

"I have no idea."

His warmth came against me again as he shifted. "You scared me for a minute."

"Sorry about that. Sometimes I'm pretty sure it'd be easier if you could read my mind."

Hunter laughed as he traced my collarbone with his lips. "What's off limits? This?" His hand trailed over my breast slowly.

I sighed, closing my eyes. "No, that's okay."

"Hmm." He peeled my shirt up, exposing my chest. His lips rolled over the swell of my breast before his hot mouth closed over my taut nipple. He sucked as his free hand tweaked my other nipple.

I moaned, running my hands along his shoulders. "That's definitely okay." My sex swelled, uncomfortable now. "I think more touching, too."

"Awfully forward of you. Naughty girl." Hunter raised me up so he could slip my shirt off. "I assume third base has nudity."

"It does now."

He went back to my nipple for a while before his hand slid gently over my belly. His mouth stilled. Then he sighed. "I can't believe we're going to have a baby. This is a strange dream. I never thought it would happen."

"I am the maker of miracles," I said, just about ready to push on the top of his head to get him where I needed him. His sentiments were sweet and all, but this girl needed a little action.

He scooted up, going the opposite way to where I wanted him to. I didn't remember being so sexually frustrated when I was a virgin.

His lips connected with mine, hot and passionate. His hand moved down to my thigh, rubbing along the outside. I clung to him, opening my legs a little. That hand was in the wrong spot!

I felt down his stomach, marveling at the muscle, before dipping into his boxers. My fingers glided along that smooth, velvety skin.

"Is that allowed?" Hunter said against my lips, his breath heavy.

"I think everything but sex is allowed."

"You're making the rules…"

"Oh, right. Then yes, everything but sex is allowed. And in the middle of the night when I randomly wake up, desperate and horny, sex is allowed."

"Cheater." He nibbled my lips as my palm worked down his shaft to the base. I took a firm hold and stroked slowly. His groan was agonized. "I don't think I'll end up liking this very much." His hand dipped into my pajama bottoms.

"Going backwards probably won't be as much fun, no. Too bad." I scooted forward, needing more of his body against mine. I took him out of his boxers, pushing the material down. His tip hit off my clothed hip.

I spread my legs, biting his lip a little when his fingers traced over my panty-covered sex. His touch was firm but light, mostly teasing. I gyrated up, something a virgin probably wouldn't do. I didn't care. I needed a little satisfaction.

I latched on to his neck with one hand and stroked harder with the other. I pulled against his neck, making him put more weight on top of me. His hand moved to the top of my panties. His fingers dug a little, and then his hand pushed back down. His skin slid over my wet sex.

"Oh God," I said, feeling the fervor.

His finger circled my nub before dipping low and then entering my body.

I moaned into his mouth, sucking in his tongue and gyrating my hips. His fingers worked in me, making the pleasure spiral inside me. I panted, tightening up. Feeling the heat.

He went back down to my nipple, sucking it in, making it impossible to stroke him. I relented for the moment, assuming he was about to explode. I knew how he felt.

His tongue circled before he sucked harder. A tiny bite of pain edged the sensation. When he backed off, the tingling amplified the pleasure, making me moan and arch up to him. His thumb manipulated my clit as his fingers plunged. The heat simmered, then boiled. My body wound up. My muscles flexed, one by one.

"Oh God." I dug my fingertips into his skin. "Oh Hunt—" I ripped apart. An orgasm tore through me without warning. I moaned into it, shaking on the bed.

As it drained, my kiss turned languid. I rubbed my hands against his hard chest before reaching down and pushing his boxers completely off. He rose up to get the job done before letting me roll him to his back.

I kissed his lips, hot and heavy, before moving down his fantastic chest. I trailed my tongue between his abs before reaching his large manhood. I circled the tip with my tongue before sucking it in, taking it as far as I could go.

Hunter's hands fisted in the sheets. His exhale was audible. I chased my mouth with my hand, bobbing on him. After a while I backed off, keeping my hand going, before swirling my tongue around his tip again. And then suction.

"Holy f—" Hunter pulled at the sheets. His magnificent arms and chest flexed, thick cords of muscle glistening in the light. I was transfixed, watching his body and completely forgetting about what I was doing.

Thank God for autopilot, even in this.

"I'm going to—" He rose and moved me off him while grabbing his boxers. He exploded into the material.

After he cleaned up a little, he reached down for me. I'd been staring with an amused grin.

"What?" he asked with a sleepy smile.

"Didn't want to deal with your handiwork when kissing me, huh?"

He chuckled as he positioned himself next to me on the bed. He turned onto his side, running his palm along my belly. "Not really. I doubted you'd mind."

He leaned into me, resuming the kissing. Deep and passionate, his lips moved over mine. His tongue wet my bottom lip as his thumb hooked into my waistband. "I'm allowed to reciprocate, right?"

"Encouraged to, yes."

"Eventually. I'm enjoying just kissing you for now."

I ran my fingers through his hair. "You don't have to spell everything out. I am capable of putting two and two together..."

"Are you sure? I played your puzzle game. I'm not sure you have a head for it."

"Oh really? Is that right?" I scoffed. "Just wait. Wait until I unleash my current creation on you. You'll cry, it's so hard."

He rose up to look down on me. His brow furrowed. His business look replaced the passion and desire from a moment before. "Are you talking about the new levels you're designing?"

It took me a second to react. I didn't like the business look interrupting our playtime. "No. Those are for the common folk. I designed some rough stuff just for you. It won't have the shine and gloss because I don't have the time, but it will make you pull your hair out. Just watch."

His hard look cleared. His expression melted back into that of love. He leaned back toward my lips.

"You're not normal, did you know that?" I said through his kisses. "Normal people can't switch off sexy times that fast."

"I've had my whole adulthood to perfect switching into my business mentality. It's only with you that I'd rather not."

"Hmm." I snuggled deeper into the pillow as I smiled, pulling him so he would move on top of me. He leaned down to finish pushing off my pants and panties, then started to comply before freezing and looking down at my stomach. "Are you sure?"

"I'm barely showing, Hunter. This is fine. You won't squish the baby."

He moved over me slowly, putting his elbows on either side of me, and no doubt bracing on his knees, to keep from resting on me fully. His kiss was sweet. "My baby."

I angled my head to get a deeper kiss. His hips turned toward me a fraction. His cock slid up my wet sex.

"Ohhh, wow." My eyes fluttered and my body purred. I tightened my legs around him.

His hips angled again. His cock slid away, and then came back again. A wave of arousal stole over me. I tried to arch, but there wasn't room. I pushed my hips back, deeper into the bed, creating some space. His tip slid down, through my nether lips. It stopped too soon.

I pulled back a little more until that blunt head put firm pressure at my opening. I paused as my nerve endings fired. Heat crashed into me. My body sizzled.

"We shouldn't do this," I said into Hunter's mouth. All humor had been erased. His smile was gone. His body was frozen over mine, braced. His lips rested on mine, waiting. He was putting all the power in my hands.

"Okay." It was barely whispered. Hardly more than a release of breath. He didn't move.

I captured his lips with mine, angling up just a fraction. That blunt tip pushed at my opening. Threatening to enter. Expectation wrapped around me, heightening this moment. My core pounded, needing him.

"I didn't want to have sex," I said again, begging him to either back off, or forgive me my inability to put on the brakes.

"I know," he said, pulling back slowly. The pressure lightened before his tip dragged along my slit.

Our breath started to labor. My body trembled under his. All my focus was on him near my opening. On this precipice of intimacy. It didn't matter that we'd done this before. It didn't matter that neither of us were virgins. Strangely, it felt like we were. This felt like that first time when we couldn't deny ourselves any longer. When we were daring each other to keep going. To make our bodies as one.

I put one hand on the back of his neck, pulling his lips harder against mine. The other hand found his back, gently, barely touching. I sucked his tongue into my mouth and slowly ground my hips toward him. His tip moved. It paused at my opening again.

I applied pressure with the hand on his back.

"Are you sure?" he asked, a small tremor in his voice.

"Yes."

His hips rocked forward marginally. His tip barely parted my folds. "I love you."

He drove forward. His manhood thrust into me, filling me up.

"Ohhmmmm." I wrapped my legs around his waist.

He pulled back and then rocked forward. I swung my hips upward. Sparks shot through my body. Pleasure unfurled like a flower, soaking into me and boiling my blood. I lost all control.

"You feel so unbelievably good," Hunter exalted, his movements silky. His body sleek.

I groaned, clutching him. I swung my hips up wildly, crashing into him as he rocked down onto me. Everything tightened. My breathing labored.

"Oh yes," I said, over and over. "Yes, Hunter." I squeezed him tightly with both my arms and legs. I held him in my body, the movements getting smaller now, but much more intense. Almost unbearable.

"Yes. Yes!" I just kept repeating it, over and over. It was like the track was skipping. Like a wire tightening around a spool, my body wound up. Pleasure coursed through me. Slapping me. Pulling.

"Come with me, baby," Hunter groaned in my ear.

Color burst behind my eyes. My body blasted apart. I shook under him, violently, the orgasm vibrating through my body.

It took me a while to come down. Each time I thought I was ready to relax, an aftershock sizzled through me. My arms and legs tingled.

"That was the stuff," I said with smile. "If only losing my virginity had been that good."

"I'm glad it wasn't, for both of us," Hunter said seriously, moving off to the side. His hand trailed across my stomach. "It makes it that much better with you. Let's tell your mom tomorrow."

"Promise you won't dump me when you go to leave and realize her hand is in your pocket?"

"I doubt she's as bad as you think."

"She's *exactly* as bad as I think, if not worse. Trust me. She's not even shy about gold digging in her old age. She goes right for it. The only guys that will give her the time of day are married."

"Desperation does strange things to people. I'll look into it. She might just be mismanaging her money."

"You don't need to, Hunter. She's not your problem. You have a crazy dad. That's enough for you."

Hunter stayed silent for a while, stroking my stomach. When he spoke next, his tone had deepened, almost sounding suspicious. "Why don't you want me to help?"

"Because...she sucks, Hunter. I told you. She's embarrassing. You're the father of my baby, but you're not tied to her. You don't have to help her. I appreciate that you want to do me a favor, but I'm not sure I want you to get involved that much with her. It's... There's no other way to describe it. It's embarrassing."

"What if we were married?"

Tingles worked through my body. This wasn't how I hoped he'd eventually bring this subject up... "You can't view marriage as a way to get into my mother's financial situation, Hunter. That's just weird. And very unromantic."

He fell silent again, still stroking my belly. Eventually he rolled out of bed, turned out the lights, and came back, all without saying a word. He curled up around me. "I love you. Good night."

"Love you." I turned so my cheek would be against his lips. He gave me a kiss before I turned back, snuggling into his arms.

My mind went back to the way he'd asked about marriage. Didn't it matter to him at all? Worse, had I just put him off, making him think I didn't want it?

Chapter 8

I AWOKE THE next morning as Hunter was opening the shades, allowing the sunlight to splash the room. I glanced at the clock. It was eight o'clock.

"What are you still doing here?" I asked in confusion. I had to think really hard about what day it was. "Today is Saturday, right?"

He turned to me, in jeans that perfectly displayed his butt and strong thighs. I knew this even though he was facing me because I'd picked them out. He was also wearing a shirt on the dressy side that did a fabulous job of showing his cut upper body, leading down to his trim hips. I'd picked that shirt out, too. I had great taste.

"I'm taking the day off," he said. "So are you. We're going to go see your mother. Among other things."

"Among other things?" I rose up to my elbow. "What things?"

"Do you want breakfast in bed, or would you rather go downstairs?"

I sat up and rubbed my eyes. "I'll go down. My taste

buds have gone berserk. I might need to forage through the kitchen until I figure out what sounds good."

Hunter didn't say anything. After a second I realized he hadn't moved either. He was staring down at me with a blank expression.

"What?" I asked, flinging the sheets off so I could get up.

"I should've known that. I've missed a lot of your pregnancy. I've been given the rare opportunity for a second chance, and I'm squandering it."

"Hey, glass-half-empty, cheer up. There's still a million months to go." I slipped on one of his shirts. They were big and he liked seeing me in them. "And no you haven't! I've seen you every day since this whole thing began. I may not work with you, but I work near you. That counts."

I tied my hair up in a ponytail. He still hadn't moved.

I went to him and slipped my arms around his waist. "Do I have time for a shower before or should I take it after?"

His chuckle splashed breath across the top of my head. "Strangely, when you don't try to make me feel better about a situation, and instead think about food, it lifts the load off."

"Food is the great cure-all. So do I have time?"

He kissed the top of my head. "Yes. I'll see you downstairs. Dress in something pretty that you like to wear."

"Something pretty that I like to wear? Cryptic."

"Something that'll impress your mother," he said as he made his way out of the room.

I got nervous flutters. I really wasn't looking forward to telling her. It would just cement the idea that now she could ask my rich baby-daddy for money.

I really hoped she didn't nudge and wink at me for trapping a rich man with a baby. It was the kind of thing she'd think. In fact, it was the kind of thing a lot of people would think, apparently. When I'd told Kimberly a month ago, she'd squealed and freaked out, as I'd expected. But then she'd said I shouldn't tell the others until I'd got a ring or there was no other choice. She worried that they'd think I planned an *oops.*

I shook it off as I climbed into the shower. There was nothing for it—I was pregnant, and today would probably suck. Best to get on with it.

A COUPLE OF hours later, Hunter paused in the garage, looking between his sports car and my Land Rover. Finally he put his hand to the small of my back to lead me to the passenger side of my Land Rover.

"I didn't say you could drive my car," I said as I climbed up into the seat.

"Can I drive?"

"What's the magic word?"

He was smiling as he got into the driver's seat. "I love you."

"That is three words. And therefore, not correct. Try

again, please." I nodded toward him. "I just gave you a hint."

He pushed the button to open the garage. His smile grew. "I love that you're the mother of my child."

"I'm not even going to count those words. Epic fail. Keep trying."

He started the car. "Last night was the best sex of my life, and it was because it was so much more than sex. I love you more than I've loved anyone, ever. You've helped me to experience the world around me, and that has allowed me a larger capacity to care. You are everything to me, Olivia."

I blinked away tears. I loved his sticky-sweet moments, when he took a look around him and realized that he'd been living a half-life all this time. He then opened up his heart and put to words all the things he felt—rare for a man.

"Wrong again," I said, putting my hand on his upper thigh.

"Please," he said, pulling out of the driveway.

"That's it! Kind of jumped the gun on the privilege, though. Next time, you might try using it *before* you drive away in my car."

"Ah. Is that how it works."

"It is indeed. Don't worry. I'll get you society-ready in no time. Next lesson, thank you."

It didn't take long to realize we were going to see my mom before the "other things" he'd mentioned. A thought struck me. His mom was out this way, too.

Maybe he finally planned to stop in and confront one of his remaining fears. We'd get my mom's blessing—hopefully—and he'd get his mom's. That would make this day much less sucky.

About a half-hour later we pulled to a stop outside of my mother's house. My heart sank when I saw her car in the driveway. I hadn't called her to say we were coming. I should have, but I really hoped she wouldn't be home.

"She's home." I opened the door as Hunter did.

"These jeans are tight. I don't think she can get her hand in my pocket." Hunter came around the car and took my hand.

"It won't be long until you know for sure, huh?"

Standing in front of her door, I knocked. Then buckled down and ran the doorbell. Maybe she wouldn't answer…

The lock disengaged.

"Damn."

The door swung open, revealing my mother, all done up and smiling. She had on a breezy, expensive-looking dress and glittering jewelry. Her hair was swept back, showing impeccable makeup on her beautiful face, looking ten years younger than her true age.

"Do you have company over?" I asked in confusion. She always did hair and makeup, but this was overkill for a Saturday morning.

"Just you!" She stepped back and gestured us in. "Welcome, Hunter. May I call you Hunter?"

"Yes." Hunter directed me in and then stepped in

behind me. He was wearing his business mask, making him somewhat curt and distant. It had the effect of simmering down my mother's exuberance. Strangely, it also calmed me. If anyone could handle my mom, Hunter could.

"Come in, come in. I was so excited to get your call. Can I get you a drink?" My mother bustled ahead of us, leading us into the living room.

"You called her? That's cheating," I muttered.

"A glass of wine, maybe?" she asked, watching as we sat. "Brandy?"

"Coffee is fine for me," Hunter said. He glanced at me.

"Water, Mom. Thanks."

"Sure. Stay right there." She glided out of the room.

"I've never been on this end of her people-pleasing side. It's weird." I leaned against Hunter as he took my hand again, threading his fingers between mine.

"I didn't plan on being here long. We can leave whenever you want."

I made as if to get up. He smiled. "Let's break the news first."

My mom came back in with a tray. She set the tray on the coffee table and distributed drinks. She offered a plate of crackers and cheese to Hunter.

He shook his head before looking at me.

"Olivia?" My mom said, moving a little closer.

"No, thanks."

She set the plate down and situated herself in the

chair across from me. Her legs crossed at the ankles and her dress swished just right. She leaned against the arm of the chair in a way that said *relaxed* and *interested in your conversation* at the same time. The woman could entertain better than anyone I'd met. She was a pro.

"We can't stay long, Mom," I started. It needed to be said.

"I'm just so happy you stopped by. I've been trying to get you over for months!" She gave us a big smile.

"Well…"

"You are really cute together, let me just say," she said.

"Thanks, Mom. So, um…" I randomly gestured. No reason for it. Just movement to dispel some of my nervousness. "We thought that you'd want to know that…I'm pregnant."

Her face froze, as though she had to stop all reaction to keep that smile plastered on. A shadow crossed her eyes as her gaze dropped to my stomach. Her facial muscles danced as a frown wrestled her pencil-thin eyebrows. Before it could win, that smile was beaming again. "Congratulations! That's great!"

She stood, all graciousness, and held out her arms. "Give me a hug. That is just great."

Her tone had changed. She had been overly exuberant before, but now it sounded like she was struggling to be optimistic. As if depression were dragging her down.

I hugged her, confused. After sitting down, I noticed that her smile had become forced. She didn't initiate the next leg in the conversation.

"I'm four months along." I took Hunter's hand.

She nodded, her smile sputtering. She looked at Hunter, and then down at her hands. "That's great."

"So…" I didn't know what to say. I expected her to ask a few questions. Instead, she picked at her dress, making sure it swirled around the chair just right, and then looked up at Hunter. Her forced smile was back.

"How is business?" she asked him.

He squeezed my hand. "Just fine. I'm ahead of where I want to be."

"Oh that's good. I hear you have a real head for business."

"I started a business," I said. "Kinda. I'm a partner. The game we created has done really well."

"Is that right?" My mom looked at me with blank, uninterested eyes. I knew this look well. I just hadn't expected to see it today.

"Yeah. I don't work for Hunter anymore," I continued. "We live together, though. I think I told you that…"

"You didn't, no. You just said you were dating him. I didn't think it would last, in all honesty." Her smile was thin. She started, then laughed. "Just because you're so fickle, honey, you know!" She laughed again, a high-pitched, uncomfortable sound. "She finally found someone who could meet her high expectations," she said to Hunter. "It's so great."

"I think we need to go, Olivia," Hunter said quietly

to me, squeezing my hand. "Your mother probably has a lot to do."

I expected my mom to resist. To engage us in conversation. Instead, she stood. "That's too bad. It was nice of you to visit, though, Hunter. Thank you guys for stopping by."

"That's it?" I asked in confusion. I had wanted to leave early, but we'd just arrived. The departure was a bit abrupt.

"What do you mean, honey? I'm so happy for you. It's just great." She didn't mean those words. I could hear it in her tone.

Taken aback, I let Hunter lead me toward the door. Once there, my mom opened it and smiled. "Good to see you, Olivia. Nice to meet you again, Hunter. Congrats. That's just great."

How many times was she going to say *great*?

"Okay. Bye, Mom…" I let Hunter direct me, utterly confused. Once in the car, I just stared at the house for a minute, in a fog. "What the heck just happened?"

Hunter started the car. "She's jealous."

"Huh?"

"She's jealous. You landed the wealthy bachelor. Didn't you say that that was her life's plan? You've done what she could not."

"Usually parents are happy when their kids fulfill their dreams."

"I don't know your mother that well, but I think you just remind her that her life's been a failure. She's tried for how many years? You accomplished it in less than one. It probably galls. It did for my father as it concerned business. He didn't try to hide his frustration like your mother did. That is a credit to her."

"When you got the better job, you mean?"

"When I left my father's company for a CEO position, yes." Hunter sped up and got onto the freeway, going in the opposite way to home. "He exploded in anger. Then threatened me. You've seen the result."

"So my parental situation is less messed up than yours, huh? You try to beat me at everything."

Hunter took my hand. "I think she'll come around. She tried to hide her disappointment. That means she cares about you."

"As much as she ever did, anyway."

"That's better than the alternative."

I couldn't argue there. His dad was terrible. I guess I now knew my mom wasn't horrible. Just…not great.

I looked out of the window for a while, but saw nothing. I had to admit that the meeting with my mom wasn't sitting well. I would rather have had her try to get money out of Hunter, in the open, than do this suffer-in-silence routine. Because she was suffering, I had no doubt. Hunter was right: she'd tried to land the rich guy all her life. All she'd had was disappointment. The one time she got close, she found out she was pregnant with a poor man's child. I'd dashed what she'd probably thought was her last hope. And now, here I was, getting it all. Getting her dream.

She probably felt like I'd robbed her.

"She's never been great to me, and sometimes I've hated her, but this sucks." I felt a rise of emotion as we parked. "I don't want her to be unhappy."

I felt Hunter's fingers run through my hair. When I turned to him, his eyes were full of love and sympathy. "We'll give her a chance to get over her disappointment, and then we'll try again. It'll work out, Livy. Okay?"

I closed my eyes, squeezing out a tear. I felt his thumb wipe across my cheek. "Your confidence is soothing."

"Are you ready for the next event of the day?"

I took a deep breath and looked around. We were at a cemetery. The cemetery where we'd buried my father.

"Why…?"

Hunter was getting out of the car.

I followed suit, more emotion springing up. He wanted to symbolically tell my dad I was pregnant. Tears came to my eyes for the second time.

"He'd really like you, you know," I told Hunter as he took my hand.

"Why is that?"

"This—all the thoughtful stuff you do. He'd know that you were taking good care of me. And that you made me happy. That was always his chief concern."

Hunter walked me up the grassy berm. As we approached my dad's tombstone, I sucked in a breath.

Growing on his plot and around the stone were sunflowers. They pointed toward the sun, welcoming me.

Filling me with memories.

"Who…?"

"I hope you don't mind—I hired a gardener to tend his plot. He was such an important man to you, I felt you'd want him looked after."

I stood in front, dumbfounded. "I don't know what to say."

"I hope I didn't step out of bounds."

I shook my head, my lip quivering. "How do you think of these things for me while still being the rudest man alive to everyone else? It doesn't make any sense." I laughed through my tears. "No, I don't mind. You didn't overstep anything. I wish I could come here more often."

"If you don't mind, I'd like to ask him a question."

Hunter stepped in front of me. Confused, because this had just become weird, I moved to the side.

"Sir," he said softly. He took a deep breath. "I wondered if I could ask your permission for Olivia's hand in marriage?"

Chapter 9

M Y WORLD BLEACHED of color for a moment as I processed what he'd said. I looked at him with incredulous eyes as my stomach flipped over.

He stood for a moment, just looking at the head-stone, before turning to me with small worry lines around his eyes. As soon as his gaze hit me, though, I could see the anxiety melting out of his expression.

The idiot wasn't sure I'd say yes! What woman on the planet would turn him down, especially one as head-over-heels as I obviously was?

"Yes," I said in a gush. Tears flooded my eyes.

A delighted smile lit up his face before his brow fur-rowed. "Eavesdropping is rude. I haven't asked you yet."

He ran his fingers under my chin before bending slowly to run his lips across mine. "Shall we go?"

He straightened up and placed his hand on the small of my back. When I didn't move, I felt a little pressure, urging me on.

"Are you serious?" I asked. I wasn't budging. "You're

going to tease me with that but hold out on the goods?"

His hand slid to my waist and pulled me into his hard body. "All good things to those who wait."

I crinkled my nose at him and let him direct me back to the car. It took everything I had not to jump up and down in utter excitement. I had to call Kimberly! She would flip her lid!

Hunter opened the car door for me and waited to assist me in.

"Could you just…" I flicked my finger toward the front of the car. "Head to your side?"

His smile combined with a confused brow furrow, like he was flashing me right now, might've been my favorite of his expressions.

I threw my arms around his neck and pulled him in for a kiss. I felt his arms come around me, just as eager. I explored his mouth with my tongue, then backed off to nibble a little, before tilting my head and going for it, infusing the moment with all the love and passion I felt. My body got light, lit on fire, and tightened up, all at the same time.

I broke away, panting. I eyed the car. How much would my belly get in the way in that confined space?

"Not in a cemetery," he murmured. His hot lips trailed down my neck. "Anywhere but a cemetery. Or a church."

He had a point.

I pulled him down to me for one last kiss before letting him step back. His eyes lingered on me, full of longing. His lips quirked, a grin threatening. He didn't say anything, though, just walked around the car to the driver's side.

I took my chance.

"*Yay!*" I quietly squealed, something only a girl could do effectively. I balled my fists and hopped around with a manic grin, delighted. Excited.

Hunter Carlisle wants to marry me!

How did I get so lucky? Seriously! There were no words!

As the last bubbles of exuberance swam up my insides, I slowed to the speed of a normal person. Hunter's door opened on the other side of the car, showing that confused grin again. Man, the guy was so freaking hot. I could not believe this was happening.

Taking a deep breath, I wiped the back of my hand across my brow, moving my hair away from my perspiring face. It was a terrible cover, but it would have to do.

"Need help?" he asked, not climbing in yet. He was probably waiting to see if I would falter getting into the car.

"Hunter, for the last time, I am pregnant, not incompetent." I climbed in. "It's not like this is a monster truck or anything."

Hunter sank into his seat, waited until I had my seatbelt on, and started her up. "How are you with fatigue?"

"In general?" I asked. To his nod, I said, "I'm actually okay. I feel good. This stage is like a second wind after you've been working out or something."

"So this is the glory time, right? The second trimester?"

I gave him a sideways glance. "Trust you to do the research. But yeah, I think so. My food aversion isn't as strong as it was, and I'm not uncomfortable. These are the glory days."

He reached across the space and put his hand on my belly. "Do you want to know the sex, or should we wait until he or she is born?"

As we headed up the freeway, I was surprised when he pulled into the lane to take us across the bridge to the East Bay. "Where are we going now?"

I scowled at him, which was ruined by the smile drifting up my face. "Fine, keep your secrets. Um…" I scratched my chin, thinking about the sex. I didn't much care if it was a girl or boy. I really hadn't thought that far ahead. "I'll probably want to know just so I can plan the colors. I hate yellow and don't want a baby decked out in all green. Pictures would be ruined with that color scheme."

"We can have everything picked out while we're in the hospital."

I frowned as we slowed for traffic to go across the Bay Bridge, both because my curiosity over where we were going was getting the better of me, and because I hadn't thought about not having to go baby shopping.

I looked at him thoughtfully, enjoying the view while I pondered how lazy I wanted to be. "I think I'd rather buy them. With you. That seems like a nice thing to do together as we get closer. Like a valve to release some of the excitement or something."

Hunter glanced over with soft eyes. He moved his hand from my bump to then thread his fingers between mine. "I agree. So we'll know the sex, then?"

"Would that be okay with you?"

"Either way is okay with me." After another moment, he said, "I wonder what he or she will look like. If…"

I squeezed his hand. "I hope he or she looks like you. You're hotter."

His chest expanded and then deflated. "It's still surreal. But I've realized something. If it wasn't mine, and you admitted that to me, I'd still want you both in my life. You could admit you're cheating with my father, were never faithful, and I'd still ask you to marry me, Olivia. I can't imagine a life without you in it. I still have moments of doubt, but that's just remembering the pain. I wouldn't turn my back like I did with Denise. I couldn't. I love you too much."

I brought our held hands to my belly. "I should record this conversation for when I gain fifty pounds and wander around in nothing but sweatpants."

"We'll get you the best sweatpants money can buy."

"Or how about when I am home all day, wading through dirty diapers and hormones, have forgotten to brush my teeth and hair—forget about a shower—and want to toss you out of a window when you ask how my day was. You'll probably think back and *wish* you hadn't broached the subject with my father."

Hunter chuckled as he pulled into a parking place on the side of the street. Lining the way were little shops and restaurants. People passed by, some in a hurry, but many meandering along, checking out the wares in the store windows they passed.

"I'll cherish those days. I'll take lots of pictures. Nothing like stress and hormones for blackmailing purposes." He winked at me before getting out of the car.

Warmth filled my chest as I followed. He had no idea what he was talking about, but it made me feel better that he wasn't scared of the beast I would probably turn into. I'd heard the stories. I'd definitely need a lot of assurance Hunter wouldn't just leave me for the line of suitors waiting at his door, hoping I'd bugger off.

Song lyrics popped into my head: "If you want to be happy for the rest of your life, never make a pretty woman your wife." Wasn't that the truth.

Hunter waited for me to get to his side before guiding me up the street. I heard my name called before Kimberly hastened toward me with a huge smile and loose, bouncing curls.

"Oh, hey!" I said, giving her a hug hello. "What are you doing here?" I looked around, suddenly realizing I didn't know where *here* was. I was pretty sure we were in the Peninsula somewhere, but the exact town eluded me.

Kimberly asked Hunter, "She doesn't know?"

"She knows my intentions, that's all." Hunter's hand slid to my waist and he pulled me in for a sideways hug. His voice took on that commanding tone that gave me shivers. "I didn't tell her about my plans for the rest of the day and ask that you don't, either."

Her eyes widened and her mouth turned into a thin line for a second. Jubilation bubbled up a moment later.

"Shall we?" Hunter asked, stepping forward.

Kimberly fell in beside me. "What did your mom say? Was she stoked?"

"No, actually." My mood dimmed as I told Kimberly about my mom's reaction. "She couldn't wait to get us out of there."

Kimberly frowned as we stopped in front of a small shop with a large diamond stenciled on the glass. My troubles with my mom evaporated for the moment. "No way…"

"Yes! And I get to help!" Kimberly grabbed my hand in both of hers and squeezed. "This is so exciting!"

"Olivia," Hunter said, his tone still powerful and commanding. I'd forgotten the walls only came down for me. Not that I minded. He was hot when he dominated the room. Or, in this case, the street. "Would you like to pick out your ring by yourself, or would you like to choose the style and let me surprise you with the details?"

"Oh my God," I said in a hasty release of breath. "This is really happening."

"I *know*!" Kimberly danced around again, still holding my hand. She didn't care that she was making a show of herself in front of Hunter...and a bunch of other strangers.

I thought about it. The storybooks all said it was great to be surprised, but I would wear it every day. I wanted something I liked. Of course, Hunter was an excellent judge of all things fashion. I could probably trust his opinion better than my own.

"Maybe I'll pick out the style," I said sheepishly.

Hunter stepped away, leaving me with Kimberly. "There is no ceiling. There are no restrictions. Pick out whatever you want, as big as you want. If you don't find something you like, we'll go elsewhere. Just text me when you're done."

"You're not coming in?" I asked. That weird fear of being left alone with a baby resurfaced. It made no sense. It came out of nowhere. My eyes filled with tears and my lip started to tremble. I stepped toward him, afraid to be left behind.

His eyes softened immediately. He took the hand I reached out toward him. The other was still held by Kimberly, who hadn't budged. I felt like a child not wanting to be carted off by the babysitter.

"I'll just go grab a cup of coffee so you can have girl time. When you're ready, I'll step in. Okay? Or would you rather I was in there with you?"

"Livy, c'mon. It'll be fun!" Kimberly stepped closer to my side. To Hunter she said, "My sister went through this when she was pregnant. It's a good sign, trust me."

Hunter didn't seem to have heard her. He was still

looking at me with those sexy eyes, waiting for my decision.

I dropped his hand and shrugged, immediately pulled toward the door by Kimberly. "I'll check in with you in a bit."

He stood there until I lost sight of him, sucked into the shop like fluff through a vacuum.

"These hormones are driving me crazy," I said to Kimberly as the glitter entranced me. "At least I hope it's hormone related. Otherwise I'm going crazy."

"I have no idea if it's a good sign—I figured saying that would help—but my sister definitely got unbalanced with the hormones. She'd randomly start crying all the time. We saw a kid hugging a puppy once and she went to pieces." Kimberly stood me in front of the solitaire section. "I cannot believe Hunter Carlisle is going to propose. I mean…he went from an arranged marriage with a woman he was never caught dead with in public to a fiancé and a father. Holy cow, Olivia, you have the magic touch!"

"I'm just as surprised as you are." I let my gaze run across all the glitter. Bursts and flares and sparkles tried to capture my attention at every turn. I leaned in to get a better look, and felt overwhelmed immediately. "I don't know where to start."

"Can I help you?" A woman with coiffed gray hair and a pleasant smile came to stand in front of us.

"Olivia, so good to see you." Mr. Porter, the man who had fitted me for a few pieces of jewelry when I first started working for Hunter, stepped out of a backroom. To the woman, he said, "She's Mr. Carlisle's soon-to-be fiancée."

The woman's smile became genuine instead of something only a customer service person would wear. "Congratulations!"

"Thanks," I said as I tucked a lock of hair behind my ear. "This is Kimberly."

"Wonderful." Mr. Porter spread his hands across the glass. "What did you have in mind?"

"We should decide on cut of diamond first." Kimberly bent over the glass, taking control.

An hour flew by like it was a few minutes. Various diamonds were brought out and placed on black mats, glittering in the overhead light. I chose a more traditional round stone, then picked out a few sizes, before browsing styles of settings. Even narrowing it down constantly overwhelmed me. I liked them all while also liking none. My opinion swung between complacent and picky. Like trying on dresses, after the first few, I stopped seeing details.

Kimberly was a champ, directing my eye and taking over the details that Hunter might have. She yayed or nayed things for whatever reasons, having Mr. Porter and his helper nod thoughtfully or in agreement. Occasionally they bickered about something or other—I had no idea what—and more often than not Kimberly would view the diamond through the magnifying glass. The woman was a pro.

Once I had a general idea of what I wanted, Kimberly nodded thoughtfully. A smile replaced a concentrated look. "Let's go get Hunter!"

I thanked the staff and left the shop, bending over my phone to text message. "I thought that would be more fun."

"You didn't have fun?" Kimberly sounded shocked.

"I did at first, but it's kind of brutal with all the specifications. Color and cut and weight—if we had a budget it would be ten times harder."

"No budget was definitely a huge perk." She sighed. "I wish Robby would finally propose. We've talked about it, but so far *nothing*. I have no idea what he's waiting for."

"You to get knocked up?"

Kimberly shook her head adamantly. "No thank you. I'm very happy for you, Livy, but I'd like a wedding and a house before I get pregnant. I want to go the traditional route. Someday."

"That had been my plan before Hunter dazzled me into being careless."

"I don't blame you. I told Nana I had to do lunch another day because Hunter Carlisle asked for my help."

I dropped my mouth open and grabbed her arm. "Kimmie! You did not."

She rolled her eyes. "Nana forgave me as soon as she heard it was Hunter Carlisle. You just don't say no to him. You'll see."

"Oh, I've seen. I'm pregnant, remember?"

We stopped talking as the man of the hour came striding down the street, wearing those jeans like he might a suit of gold. His broad shoulders swung with each step. His chiseled, handsome face drew the eyes of the passersby. And he was all mine. Or soon would be.

If it was possible for a heart to sigh, mine just did.

"Hey, baby," I said as he came to stop beside me.

He bent down, still in business mode before touching his lips off mine. It was very odd. "Did you find something you liked?"

I rocked my head from side to side. "Kinda. There were too many options. I narrowed it down for you, though."

Hunter started forward toward the shop.

"Do you…want me to go?" Kimberly asked hopefully.

Hunter glanced at me as he held the door. He didn't say anything or make any sign that he had heard her, waiting for me to make the decision.

I couldn't help chuckling. This man, ignoring my friend, was the same guy who had taken it upon himself to arrange for the upkeep of my father's plot. He was the same guy who had told me he didn't want to live without me; who had planned this day, which was already one of the best of my life. It was comical when you could see it from both sides.

"She's pretty helpful," I told him.

"After you," Hunter said in a brusque tone.

Kimberly beamed as she walked through the door,

followed by Hunter. And then I was left standing on my own in the middle of the sidewalk. I hadn't really thought that through.

Fifteen minutes later I was leaning against the wall when Kimberly sauntered out, followed by Hunter. He had a small bag in his hand.

"That was quick," I said, pushing away from the wall.

"You should've waited in a café, Livy," Kimberly said. "It's in bad taste to see him leaving with the merchandise."

What kind of weird rule was that? I knew what he went in there for. I was too old to believe in Santa Claus.

"Shall we?" Hunter asked me, putting out his hand to herd me toward the car.

"Now what?" I asked as we got to the Land Rover and Hunter opened my door.

"Okay, I'll talk to you later, Livy!" Kimberly waved as she stepped away. "Thanks for letting me take part, Hunter."

I said goodbye to Kimberly, eager to find out what was next. He let me know his intentions, he had the hardware…so would he do this now, or maybe we'd finally face his fears and tell his mom…

Chapter 10

"DID YOU PLAN all this last night?" I asked Hunter as he headed toward the city.

"We should have this conversation later."

I frowned at him, but his business mask was still on, not thawed from dealing with people yet. I reached out my hand. Without hesitation, he switched hands on the steering wheel and took it, letting me pull it in to my lap. His eyes softened immediately. That was all it took.

I felt smug and figured I might as well just wait it out. He was like a steel trap. If he didn't want to tell me what was coming next, he wouldn't. I didn't think so, anyway. I would have to test that theory someday.

After a slow drive through the city and all its traffic, and followed by a faster drive across the Golden Gate Bridge, Hunter turned off and followed the road to the place where I'd first accepted his job offer.

My heart started beating wildly.

When he parked, and I saw Bert's car, my breath came short. It felt like a five-hundred-pound man was sitting on my chest. And then we walked up that familiar path through the trees, hand in hand, and I saw the very picnic table we'd sat at, with the same meal laid out, tears came to my eyes. It was the first time I'd said yes to him. The first time in a long string of yeses that had led to this day. To this moment.

"Mr. Ramous, that'll be all," Hunter said as we stopped beside the table.

"Yes, sir." Bert gave me a huge smile and a big thumbs-up before heading back toward his car.

I turned to Hunter as if in a dream. Everything slowed down as he lowered to one knee, the little black box in his outstretched hand. His sexy gaze took me in and connected in a deep and intimate way, holding me.

He opened the box, displaying a ring and setting I hadn't even seen in that store. The band and diamond were classic and traditional but with an artistic flair that caught and trapped my eye. The glitter blurred as my eyes filled with tears of complete happiness.

"Olivia, I brought you here because this is where I fell in love with you. This is where I saw a woman, naive in business, without much more than a dime to her name, turn me down. You tried to walk away because I didn't live up to your high and exacting standards. I trapped you that day. I outmaneuvered you. And more, I bent farther than I have with anyone, and learned that compromise wouldn't break me. Following your every whim won't break me. Only losing you could accomplish that. Losing you would destroy me."

He turned my hand over and kissed my palm. "Olivia Jonston, will you do me the greatest honor and be my wife?"

"Yes!" I said, tears dripping down my cheeks. "Yes, Hunter!"

He stood and took the ring from the box before gently threading it onto my finger. "This diamond will have to be switched out for one with a better cut and clarity, but he couldn't accomplish that today. I didn't want to wait to ask you."

"I wouldn't have wanted to wait either. And this one is perfect!"

He kissed me, holding me tight. After a moment he backed away and led me to the table. "Are you hungry?"

I blew out a breath, still crying. My makeup was probably all over my face. I wiped under my eyes and let Hunter put food on my plate.

"This is perfect, Hunter. You couldn't have chosen a better spot."

He sat opposite me, his face so different from the last time he'd sat there. So much more relaxed, his gaze more open. We'd come a long way in a short amount of time.

"Sorry about all the driving," he said as he spooned potato salad onto his plate. "I did organize this at the last minute. It was your comment about your mother that struck a chord. I've been selfishly holding off asking you to marry me because I wanted to do it differently than the last time. I wanted the events to be different."

"What do you mean?"

"With Denise, I found out she was pregnant, I proposed, and then I found out everything was a sham. This time, I didn't want to follow that same order."

I swallowed my bite. "You wanted to make sure it wasn't a scam before you proposed, you mean?"

A guilty look crossed his face. "At first, I admit that yes, that had crossed my mind. But then, after our scare, I realized that it really didn't matter. I want you. I know you love me—you're very open about your feelings. It was at this bench, looking at you then as I'm looking at you now, that I realized I'd do anything to get you. I'd pull any strings, I'd ruin any deal—I'd rearrange my way of doing things to secure you.

"After that, I put it to the back of my mind until I had some other things sorted out. It took your comment last night to jog me out of my planning. You are so incredibly patient, Olivia. You trust me blindly. You stick by me through the worst of my moods, and the most arduous of my needs. You deserved more than to be kept waiting."

I watched my ring sparkle in the spotted light as the sun broke through the canopy. "Worth the wait."

"You are so worth the wait. You are worth a life of cold business until I could meet you."

I eyed the sparkling wine in front of me dubiously.

"It's sparkling apple cider. While the French partake in wine during pregnancy, I'm not sure we need to."

"No argument there." I took a sip, feeling a sense of peace and happiness wash over me.

"We could've taken today's trip in a different order, but I wanted to tell your mother before I proposed," he said before taking a bite of his sandwich.

"You didn't want me to think you were buying your way into her finances?" I huffed out a laugh. "Marriage is a steep price to pay for that kind of privilege."

"I think it was probably a good idea, in hindsight, seeing how she reacted."

"She probably thinks I trapped you."

"That's another thing that occurred to me." His voice took on an edge. "Kimberly mentioned how some people might view our situation. I've been slack about meeting your friends. I apologize for that. I've let my business affairs rule me recently."

"I can tell you're planning something right now. You always get more eloquent and correct when you're strategizing."

His eyes twinkled. "Anyway. The day isn't over. That's what I am getting at."

"You're going to meet my friends?" I asked with an incredulous flutter to my words. "Well…the people I occasionally hang around, anyway. I really do need to get out more."

"After this we'll meet them for drinks. I wanted that ring on your finger before we did. I trapped you. I want that to be common knowledge."

I just shook my head. He was too good for me. "I feel like I'm living in a dream."

"I've put you through enough nightmares for a lifetime."

He hadn't, but I didn't plan to say it.

Constantly smiling and looking at my finger while trying to eat was surprisingly difficult. I made it happen, though. Like a champ.

When we were done, and after we had taken a moment just to hold hands and be in each other's presence, Hunter walked with me back to the car. He told Bert we'd finished, had Bert take a few pictures to mark the occasion, and then opened my door for me. As he was about to close me in, he said, "And I should warn you. I invited Jonathan. I intend to make my claim on you public."

A wave of shivers rolled through me. Hunter Carlisle did nothing by halves. I wondered what kind of statement he intended to make, and if I should have the cops on standby.

Chapter 11

HUNTER TOOK ME home to get changed for whatever finale he had planned. After letting him pick out my clothes, knowing that he had something in mind and wanting him to just take control to suit his own ends, I refreshed my makeup and curled my hair a little. The "no heels" rule was still in effect, but I did get away with wedges. Or maybe he just didn't notice, because the dress he picked out for me showed, pretty obviously, my baby bump. Every time I was in his sight he glanced at it, and then came closer to rest his hand on my stomach.

Around dinnertime we pulled up in front of a swanky hotel in downtown San Francisco. The name said it was French and the valet in a suit said it was ritzy. Hunter planned to splash some money around; I had no doubt. He knew what would impress these people.

Hunter checked in with the host. "The Carlisle party."

The man checked his list and said, "Yes, of course. The upstairs area is ready for you. Guests have already arrived."

Hunter turned toward the back of the restaurant, directing me through the people and up the stairs. As we crested the floor, white-topped tables decorated with flowers greeted me. Light glowed from crystal chandeliers, cascading down onto the wood floor dotted with plush rugs. Servers wandered through the twenty or so people with hors d'oeuvres. At the far end of the room, between two pillars, stood the bar.

People turned our way. I saw familiar faces immediately. Kimberly and Robby were there, Kimberly smiling like a child on Christmas morning, Jen and Rick, Jett with some woman I didn't know, and, of course, Tera and Jonathan. The rest were older people; one who was a ginger just like Kimberly—her dad, probably. Most looked grim and wore ties, as if they were at a business meeting.

"I felt you stiffen—what's wrong?" Hunter asked, stopping. It was no secret to me that he did not generally care about other businesspeople on a personal level. He'd turn around and leave right now if I asked him. As such, he didn't care that they were now waiting for him to enter his own party. I knew he'd make them wait as long as he wanted. I also knew no one would bat an eye.

"It's just—this is great," I said in a quiet voice. "Don't get me wrong. It's lovely. It's just, you didn't want to invite Bert or Brenda or anyone?"

He slid his hand around my waist, pulling me into him as he faced everyone again. "This is a party for the gossips and the business elite. Up until now, people have only seen you by my side as my admin. I want them to see you now as my future wife. I have a couple more months before I should be freed up significantly. I'll take you out a lot more then. This is just to make my choice known, so to speak." We started forward again. "With all you had to endure with Blaire, I don't want people gossiping about you. Wondering. I want it very clear how I feel about you. I do not want you to be compared to her in any way."

My heart swelled.

"Hi, Livy! Let me see." Kimberly grabbed for my hand as soon as we were close. Jen stepped closer with her, bending over my new ring.

"It's beautiful." Jen's hand drifted toward her chest. She glanced behind her at Rick. When she turned back, she made a face. "No point showing him."

"Why, what happened?" Kimberly asked.

Jen shrugged as Tera peered over Jen's shoulder to look at the ring. "Nothing, but let's be honest—it's not going anywhere. We fight more than we get along."

Kimberly sighed, looking at the ring with longing. "Yeah. I guess there's no point in showing Robby. I have no idea what's taking him so long."

"Tell him he'd better propose or you're going to leave him," Jen said with heat in her voice. "You've been together for years. It's time."

"I don't want to." Kimberly glanced miserably back at Robby, who was talking to the other guys. "He's probably not ready."

"Or he's just being lazy," Tera said. "Guys don't rush to slap a ring on it unless they have a reason. When's the due date, Livy?"

I felt Hunter's arm stiffen. All three girls looked up at him, almost at the same time. They must've felt the shift in his presence, or maybe his stature. He'd gone from patient and content to be near to me, to dominating the space. His hard, unwavering gaze was fixed on Tera.

Tera visually gulped. "You are pregnant, right?" she asked in a demure voice I'd never heard before. "You've always been in shape, and that dress just looks like—"

"We're expecting, yes." Hunter placed the emphasis on *we*. "I should've asked if she wanted to get married before trying to conceive, but in my mind we were already married. I failed her in that."

"I've heard a lot of people having babies without marrying," Jen hastened to say.

"You were already living together," Kimberly said.

"No, yeah. Totally. I wasn't saying…" Tera's words trailed off as she withered within Hunter's continued stare.

"I think it's great," Jen said. "When are you going to get married?"

She was looking at Hunter, but instead of answering, he looked down at me and gave a small squeeze. Apparently it was my show as far as the wedding was concerned.

I thought about it for a second. "Probably after the

baby is born. Finding a dress to fit a pregnant lady can't be easy."

"I agree. Besides, you don't want people to think it's a shotgun wedding." Jen gave Tera a nasty look.

"Shall we get a drink?" Hunter asked. I smiled at the girls and let him lead me to the bar. "What can I get for you? Sparkling water, juice…"

"Just normal water is fine."

"Hunter!" A graying man who hadn't done a great job of stuffing his large belly into his suit wandered over with a glass of brandy and an important swagger. "I heard the news." He winked and tapped the side of his nose. "Big change, huh? No one saw *that* coming."

"The news hasn't been made public yet." Hunter didn't even look at the man. Instead, he ordered drinks and looked out over the crowd, many of whom were shooting glances back his way.

"Oh come on, you didn't think news that big would stay quiet, did you?" He laughed in obnoxious ha-ha-has. "The rumor is that you screwed the pooch with that buyout and are getting out of Dodge before the shit hits the fan."

Could the guy have used any more clichés?

"Not at all. Everything is set up perfectly with the buyout. It went smoothly." Hunter took the glasses from the bartender and handed me a water. He replaced his hand around my waist and directed us away from the man without so much as a glance.

"What news?" I asked, ignoring how rude he was being. That man was annoying. Hunter's cold shoulder was good enough for him.

I got a guarded glance. "I told you—I'm making changes to be more available to you and the baby. And I'm following your lead. I'm finding something that I love, instead of worrying about being more successful than my father."

"The CEO position was to be better than your father?"

Hunter stopped near a few men in suits and ties standing with women of their own age. The men stood with pushed-back shoulders and too much ego. These guys were probably VPs or CEOs of other companies.

"In part."

"So what are you going to do instead?" I asked as Jonathan sauntered over. Speaking of too much ego. The guy was so impressed with himself it was absurd.

"I'm going to build, Livy."

"Like…construction?"

"Mr. Carlisle," Jonathan said as he reached us. Rick and Robby had grins on their faces, watching Jonathan try to speak to Hunter. "I'm so glad you invited me to this event. You have a great girl."

Hunter looked away. "I know."

Jonathan smiled at me in a way that said I could've been anybody. As long as I was standing next to Hunter, I was worth talking to. I'd lost my identity as Olivia, and gained the identity of Hunter's fiancée. It was half great, because he wouldn't be bothering me, but half disconcerting. The man was all about himself. He would push over the Pope if it meant he would get ahead.

"I'm not sure if you were aware, but I graduated from Stanford University..." Jonathan gave Hunter a smug smile.

"I'm aware. Barely a C average, correct?" Hunter asked in his business tone.

Jonathan shifted uncomfortably. He coughed into his fist. "The schedule was pretty rigorous, yes. But since graduating I've made some significant advancements in the industry."

"You're still in an entry-level position, isn't that right?" Hunter gave Jonathan a disinterested glance.

"Well...for now, yes. But I've been guaranteed a promotion as soon as a position becomes available."

"Your father arranged that, I believe..."

Jonathan shifted again. Clearly this conversation wasn't going as he had thought it would. "Well, that's just it. I'd love to get out of his shadow. You know something of that. In fact, we share a lot of the same motivations. And, you know, a lot of the same likes..." The glance at me said volumes.

And I thought I'd had a terrible interview with Hunter. Jonathan was looking to get punched.

"I definitely think I could be an asset to you," Jonathan hastened to say as Hunter turned to stare at him full-on. "I could be your eyes on the inside, as they say."

"I told you he was looking for a job," I murmured to Hunter.

If Jonathan heard, he gave no sign, and he certainly didn't appear bashful, as he should have.

An edge crept into Hunter's voice. "I am handing over the reins. I'm sure you'll hear all about it sometime tonight. I've officially resigned and a replacement has already been found."

"Wait, *what*?" I blurted. "You're that far along in your change? How come you didn't mention it?"

"That is...surprising," Jonathan said. His back straightened somewhat. "If I might ask, what comes next?"

Hunter gave me a sideways glance. His body against me tensed. "I'm going into business with Livy."

"Wait...*what*?" I stepped away from him so I could look him full in the face.

"That gaming thing?" Jonathan smirked. Hunter had devalued himself in Jonathan's eyes, it seemed. He'd certainly lost his usefulness. "Huh."

"Excuse us," Hunter said to Jonathan before steering me away to a quiet corner. "I was going to tell you differently. I hadn't realized the news had leaked already."

"What news?"

"I'm a partner in your business with Bruce. I've been planning the various releases, the business setup, our long-term goals...I'll be stepping into the CEO role after I get it off the ground. I want to build our own company, Livy. I want to do it with you."

I'd thought over all the little bits of knowledge

Hunter always seemed to have about how the game was doing. Then the confidence Bruce had. He'd been *positive* the marketing approach would be a success. I'd thought it'd just been ego, but it hadn't been. He'd known Hunter was planning it, and he thought Hunter's approach would be a sure bet.

He'd been right. The game was becoming a phenomenon. The next Candy Crush. Money was pouring in, reviews were great, and avid fans were clamoring for more.

I'd already suspected Hunter had a toe in the waters, but I'd largely thought it was being nosy. Nope. He was running the show. He was planning our future.

"When did you decide this?" I asked in a slow, deep tone. I wasn't sure how I felt about this yet.

"I fell into the decision, more than anything. I knew I'd have to change things in order to be the father I want to be. Then I saw your passion, and Mike made that comment at my mother's dinner—I've been looking for something where I can build from the ground up. That's about when Bruce asked me for advice. He had such faith in his and your design concepts. He knew the business would take off like his last one did. And he knew he couldn't handle it when it did. I just helped at first, but then...I fell into it. I found the passion I saw in you. Everything just kind of...unfolded."

"Why didn't you mention it?"

Hunter ran his thumb along my chin before kissing my lips softly. "I wanted you to choose that job over working for me. I wanted you to make the first move. You took much longer than I anticipated, though, so I got nervous you'd be...less than thrilled I was running the company without telling you. I've been trying to find the words."

"You were a coward."

A ghost of a smile crossed his lips. "You have the authority to fire me. I didn't want to push you to it."

I ran my hand up his chest. I wasn't mad. Not at all. In fact, I was relieved. "I get to work for you again."

"You don't mind?"

"No! That's why I took so long to leave. It was you."

He kissed me again. "That's what I was hoping. I've organized the company in such a way that I shouldn't have to put in a full week for a while. Not for a couple years, at least. I've delegated a lot between the three of us, and various assistants. If the company grows, though, which I'm certain it will, I can easily step down to a less demanding role while still holding the reins."

"We have a hit now, but we might not in the future. How can you possibly know it will work out?"

"Because it has to. You are the key to my happiness. For you, I'll do anything. I knew that this company was your future, so I needed to make it mine as well. This is the life I've always wanted, Livy." He ran his lips across mine again. "Are you sure you're not angry?"

I laughed and snuggled into him. "No. When do you officially start?"

"The board has decided on my replacement, so I'll be

making the transition over the next couple months, and then I'm all yours."

"I'm not going to be your admin, though…"

He laughed and took my hand. "Brenda is coming with me. She'll continue to be my assistant. I have no need for a second."

"That little—" I made a fist and shook it. "She knew about all this and didn't mention it."

"I asked her not to."

"I don't care. She's going to get a knuckle sandwich for keeping this big a secret from me. Chicks before dicks!"

Hunter led me back to the others. I said, "Just so you know, I don't require the wearing of pants in my office."

"Will you enforce a personal contract?"

"Maybe." I smiled as my chest warmed. Then my smile wilted as we fell into the company of the business-men.

Thank God we could leave guys like that behind!

The rest of the night was fabulous because I sat at the table for dinner with Kimberly, Jen, and the guys. We laughed and talked. Even Tera and Jonathan didn't ruin the mood. Hunter was by my side every second, often touching me, and occasionally rubbing my belly and kissing me. If anyone doubted that he loved me going in, they didn't by the time the night was over. He doted on me constantly, making the girls at the table sigh in envy.

A thought struck me toward the end of the night. I remembered how much I owed Kimberly for getting me the interview with Hunter, but also for always helping me when I needed it. I saw the opportunity to reciprocate.

"Hey, Hunter," I said quietly as we waited for our coats. "I wondered if you could lean on Robby to propose to Kimberly. I know it's totally not a guy thing to do, but those guys are all afraid of you. If you mentioned it, maybe he'd finally pop the question."

Hunter stared at me for a moment, probably processing that crazy request. His soft snort ruffled my hair. He looked around before a tiny smile wrestled his lips. "Only you would ask for something as awkward as that for me to accomplish. Why couldn't you be the type to be happy with money?"

I laughed and leaned into him. "You owe her, too. Without her, we never would've met."

Seriousness stole his expression. His gaze traveled my face. "You're right. Consider it done."

"I mean…but don't be obvious about it. Don't make him think she wanted you to ask."

His grin was back. "Anything else?"

"Well, you know, be cool. Don't go in hot. Just…like…ease it into the conversation. Somehow."

He squeezed me. "I'll take care of it."

I let him put my coat on and steer me toward the exit. The day had been one of bliss. Except for the small hurdle with my mother, everything had been perfect. I was engaged to the best man in the world, in a job I loved, and the life of my dreams. There was just one thing left to do. Hunter had to face his greatest fears and tell his mother.

Chapter 12

I CLOSED MY computer with a click and stretched, working out my tense shoulders. I had another day, at most, before this latest batch of levels would be done. I was working at breakneck speed.

I regretted telling Hunter that it was fine that he was my boss again. He was way more demanding than Bruce, and now that he could, he was calling the shots. He'd tell me what needed to be done, by when, and then that I shouldn't stress.

What?

"I'm going to grab a sandwich, want anything?" I asked Hunter. He didn't bother looking away from his computer. After a moment of silence, I said, "Hello?"

He still didn't look up.

Shaking my head, and deciding just to get him something anyway, I made my way out of his office. To Brenda I said, "I'm still not talking to you, but do you want a sandwich?"

She leaned back in her chair. Her face was lined with

fatigue. She was trying to get everything done and ready for Hunter to leave this job, and her with him. She was just as stressed out as he was. "Yeah. Turkey. Everything on it. Are you getting something for Hunter?"

"Yeah. Although when I asked if he wanted something, he ignored me."

"The new guy comes in tomorrow. He has a huge list of things he wants to get drawn up. Strategies or whatever. The new girl isn't cutting it." Brenda looped a thumb in the air, aimed at the empty desk next to her. "Hunter made her cry yesterday. He wasn't even being demanding."

"Yikes. Where was I?"

Brenda waved me away. "Taking your time coming into work. As usual."

"I don't work here, FYI."

"Excuses." Brenda leaned toward her computer, back to work.

I smirked and headed out, going to the sandwich shop down the street. Ten dollars for a sandwich was ridiculous, but they were good and it was close. As I was leaving our building, I heard, "Oh, Olivia!"

Confused, because I didn't recognize the voice, I stopped and looked around. An older lady was strolling toward me. My stomach dropped when I realized who it was.

"Oh, hi, Mrs. Carlisle." I licked my lips and glanced at the doors I'd just come out of. Would it be weird if I darted back inside to hide?

My next glance went to my pregnant belly. My top was strained and kind of tight. I was a walking secret reveal.

"It's so nice to see you," Hunter's mom said as she stopped in front of me with a smile. She held a Nordstrom bag.

We weren't very close to the shopping area. She'd come to this building specifically.

"Are you going to duck in to see Hunter?" I asked, playing it cool. That involved brushing back my hair and controlling my shifty eyes. I wasn't doing a good job with the eye bit.

"Yes. In part. Are you headed out?"

"Oh." I vaguely pointed down the sidewalk. "I was just going to get a sandwich. He's in there, though. If you want to say hi…"

"I wouldn't want to bother him. I could use some lunch." Only a Carlisle could make inviting herself along when she wasn't wanted still seem gracious.

I hesitated, wanting to say no and having no idea how. Then I couldn't, because she took my arm like we were longtime friends and gently tugged me in the direction I'd been heading.

Now I knew where Hunter got it.

"I haven't seen you in quite some time. I was worried that something might have happened," Trisha said with a light tone.

"Oh no. Nope. We've just been busy."

"Yes, my son always is. He makes time for you,

though, I hope?"

"Yes, he does. Or tries, anyway. He has given his notice and is about to switch jobs."

"I know. I heard. Is this the right way?"

I'd stopped paying attention. "Oh. Uh…" Could I be any less eloquent? "This way." I turned to the left at the intersection.

"I was surprised. He's built his life around that high-powered profession. I figured something big must've come up."

I couldn't tell if she thought that was a good thing, or a bad. "He just figured that he didn't want to keep up the hours," I stammered.

"Uh hmm."

We walked for a moment in silence, which felt like she was yelling, "I'm onto you!" My muscles were all quivering with nervousness. Beads of perspiration collected on my forehead.

Why hadn't she commented on the ring, currently a few inches from her arm wrapped around mine? Or the obvious baby bump announcing her grandchild? Should I have brought it up? Because I wasn't gonna!

"I've tried to get Hunter and you over for dinner," Trisha said in that light tone. She pointed at a coffee shop. With barely a nudge, we were walking into it and waiting in line.

How did she *do* that?

"Yeah, we've just been so busy." *And he's afraid to see you.* "Hopefully we can come around soon…" *When he straps on a pair of balls and faces his fears...*

When we got up to the cashier, Trisha ordered a mocha, and then asked me, "Would you like a herbal tea or something?"

An herbal tea. Because I wasn't supposed to have caffeine.

She knew.

"I'm fine. Really. I was just going to get some sandwiches..." I smiled at the cashier. Within that smile was a plea for help.

Trisha paid and steered me toward the area to wait for her beverage. "I was worried. He was so eager to have me meet you, and then he fell off the face of the earth. But I see you two are still going strong..."

I could hear the light question in her voice. She wanted me to admit my status. Clearly she wasn't a believer in outing people.

Her bad. I didn't care how awkward it got; I wasn't going to give Hunter away any more than the obvious signs she already saw. And he put those there. It wouldn't be my fault.

"Yes, we're doing well."

"Him leaving his job—big changes. How is he coping?"

She got her coffee and tried to steer me toward a table. Another wave of nervous perspiration broke out. I felt like a trapped animal.

"Oh. I...need sandwiches..." I stepped toward the door, feeling like the rudest person alive by ignoring that polite tug of hers.

"Of course." Her hand looped more securely through my arm. We might've been chums who'd known each other forever.

How the hell could I get out of this? It felt like my skin was crawling with how awkward I felt. Surely this was worse than waterboarding. Where did she train for this social torture, in a prison camp?

"Did I hear right in that you've left his employ?" she asked as we neared the sandwich shop.

I nearly groaned with the size of the line. "I did, yes."

"I saw the game you were working on. It was doing extremely well. And well positioned in the market. Your company seems well set up. Someone experience must have helped, since your other business partner lost control of his first business, correct?"

I ground my teeth. She'd done her research, and she knew damn well that Hunter was one of those business partners. God help Hunter. This woman did not like the cold shoulder. And this was just the information she was bringing up! What did she know that she was too polite to mention?

Hunter hadn't learned what he knew from his dad; he'd learned it from this woman. And I wasn't sure that he'd surpassed the teacher yet.

"I pretty much just deal with the coding and design," I said with a shaking voice, *willing* the line to move faster. "Bruce handles everything else. I have my hands full."

"Yes. And you're doing a remarkable job. How is living with my son?"

I choked on my spit. She was starting to get bolder. "Good. Really good. I had to move in after Blaire ruined my flat. Or...you know, his flat. That I was living in."

"Yes. She's under house arrest—"

Trisha cut off as I stepped up to give my order. Sandwiches tumbled out of my mouth but I wasn't really paying attention. Her gaze had dipped to my stomach. A look of pleasure took over her expression. When she glanced back up, her eyes were twinkling in a knowing way.

Damn it!

I looked like an alcoholic trying to recover, judging by how badly my hands were shaking. I paid and stepped to the side, about ready just to run. Just sprint out of the store, the sandwiches be damned. Hunter was going to kill me.

"May I see the ring?" Trisha asked with a slight smile.

"Oh. Um." She probably thought I wasn't educated with my guttural, one-syllable comments. "Yes, sure."

I held up my hand for her inspection. She took it and bent over the ring, her smile growing. When she let go, her eyes were slightly glistening. "It's beautiful. Thank you."

"Thanks." Should I say *you're welcome*? What was she thanking me for?

"I'll leave you to your sandwiches. Please tell Hunter

that I'd love to talk to him soon."

I blinked at her back as she strolled away.

What just happened?

I got the sandwiches and made my way to the office in a fog. I had no doubt now that she knew everything that was going on in Hunter's life. Maybe she'd heard about us from the party the night before, or God knew where, and now she'd verified it all.

So what would she do with the info?

I put Brenda's sandwich on her desk.

"I don't see any writing saying 'no mayo'..." She quirked an eyebrow at me.

"I just ran into Hunter's mom."

Brenda's eyes widened. She smirked. "How'd that go?"

"He hasn't told her the news." I eyed his door with a sinking feeling in the pit of my stomach.

"So I should expect a very messed-up sandwich? Since you clearly ousted him. Why not just wear a shirt that says, 'Baby in here.' And that ring is massive. You walk lopsided with that thing weighing down your hand."

I scowled at her, unable to help my smile. "The ring isn't *that* big." She scoffed. "But yes, she definitely knows. It's not like I could've hidden it."

"You better go tell him before she calls to congratulate him. He doesn't like those kinds of surprises."

"Thank you, Professor Obvious."

"You're welcome. And then you better go home, because when he realizes you messed up his sandwich, he's going to be pissed."

"I'll have the ability to fire you, you know. Bear that in mind…"

Brenda laughed and unwrapped her sandwich. Apparently she wasn't worried.

I edged into Hunter's office. I took a moment to marvel at his handsome face and his broad shoulders before I just threw it out there. "I just saw your mom. She knows everything." His head snapped up. "Like…everything. You switching jobs, organizing the company—I'm pretty sure she knows your daily schedule. She's kind of terrifying in a really soft sort of way."

Hunter entwined his fingers and stared down at his desk. "I've ignored her last couple of calls. This was bound to happen."

"She was stalking me, wasn't she? She was waiting for me to come out of the building."

Hunter rose from his desk. "Probably. I'm sorry about that."

"I didn't tell her anything, but…" I pointed at my stomach.

"I know."

"And…" I pointed my ring at him. "She came out and asked about living with you. But I didn't admit you were involved in the business. I tried to keep your secrets, Hunter."

He wrapped his arms around me and squeezed me close. "Thanks for trying. She's good at finding out about my life. She doesn't like me getting too far out of her reach."

"You couldn't have mentioned that before? That's something I would have liked to see coming."

He ran his lips across mine before stepping away to stand at the windows. He looked out in silence. I could see the tension working into his shoulders. He was probably thinking about the last time he'd told her about knocking up a woman and then proposing. How badly that had gone was probably rolling around in his head.

"At least she's happy about it," I said in a qualifying tone. "That's something, at least."

"She seemed happy?"

"The woman practically pressured me into getting knocked up. She didn't even know me then and she wanted—" I cut off when Hunter turned toward me quickly. Those sexy, smoldering eyes were trained on me. "What?"

"What did she tell you?"

I made a duckbill with my mouth in thought. Did I not tell him that little peccadillo? "It was at that party a while ago. Seriously, did I not tell you this? Because I thought I had…" At his continued, intense look, I said, "Yeah, she hinted I should give you a baby. She showed me your paintings, said you should've gotten outdoors more often, and then said you could live again through a baby. It was pretty clear she was giving me the green light to get knocked up."

"She said that?" Hunter's voice was barely more than

a whisper. His expression turned incredulous.

"Yeah. I thought it was weird. And she smiled when she looked at the ring. I think she's happy, Hunter. Or else she hides disappointment extremely well. Which...I wouldn't put past her, now that I think about it."

"You're sure?"

I tilted my head at him in confusion. I'd always thought him not wanting to tell his mother was a fear thing. Like he didn't want to admit that he was repeating his past. I had no idea the fear was linked to him thinking his mother might not approve.

I thought back to the meeting of only moments ago. To her smile, her delight, and the glossy eyes. No, she was definitely a happy grandma.

"I think you should tell her," I said softly, going to him and running my hands up his chest. "Let her experience being a grandma from the beginning with her only son. She'll definitely take it better than my mom did."

His look still intense, he glanced behind me. Then, without a word, he was striding away toward the door.

"I didn't mean *right now,*" I said.

He leaned out the door and said a few words, but I didn't catch them. A moment later, he stepped back inside and closed the door. Then locked it.

A thrill went through me.

His pace back was slow and stealthy, like a predator about to take down a sure meal. His eyes raked over me. In that commanding voice I craved, he said, "Get on your knees."

Chapter 13

———

M Y KNEES CRACKED against the floor I dropped so fast. My sexy systems roared to life, wanting him to take me with a desire so intense I couldn't think straight. My breath came fast as his powerful strides brought him closer. He stopped right in front of me and undid his pants. His large manhood bobbed out.

"Suck my cock."

I reached for him in fervor, loving this. Loving when he commanded me like this. It was so sexy and naughty. He'd mostly stopped doing it once I got pregnant. I'd missed it.

Dripping with desire, my smile showing my excitement, I crawled forward on my knees and took that velvety skin in my hand. I licked the tip before sucking it in, taking it deep.

"Look at me."

I did as he said, stroking with my hand in time with my mouth, pleasuring him. I worked my other hand under my skirt and into my panties, manipulating myself in time to his small hip thrusts. My body wound up immediately.

"Hmmm," I said as my lips glided over his hard length. My finger rubbed, my other hand stroked. I went faster as he shrugged out of his jacket and then unbuttoned his shirt. His delicious chest came into view, those defined pecs leading down into a perfect set of abs.

I worked harder, the visual fanning my arousal higher. I took him deep and then backed off, sucking as I did. Then back, my mouth taking him in greedy gulps.

"Yes, Olivia." His words weren't much more than an exhale.

I worked myself harder as I took him in faster. I stroked with my mouth, swirled with my tongue and then sucked him back in. Over and over. My body was getting ready, so tight. Wound up.

"Liv—"

I came at the same time he did, the orgasm crashing through my body and making me forget what I had been doing a moment before. As the waves of pleasure subsided, I realized that was probably a really bad thing.

"I've always said I wouldn't let you come on my face. Ew." I held my sticky hands in front of my face to hide the evidence of the final event. I really needed to pay more attention.

"Go to the bathroom and get cleaned up," Hunter instructed. His voice was softer, but that hard command still rode his words. "I want to fuck you."

"Yes, sir," I said, giddy. I practically ran to the bathroom giggling like a lunatic. After a quick clean, I stripped out of my clothes. Why not?

When I went back in, I saw that he had done the same thing. He was completely naked, standing by his desk. "This is the last day where we'll be alone in this office. Tomorrow I'll be starting to hand it over to someone else. I want to fuck you on every available surface."

Again, why not?

Smiling, I walked toward him, seeing his gaze dip to my growing belly.

"Fuck, I love you, Olivia." His voice had significantly softened. "It's hard to maintain the more severe tone you love when I see that baby, though."

"Just talk dirty and tell me to do things."

"Come here."

The now soft command trickled down my spine. Feeling light, I stood in front of him. He palmed my breast before feeling down to my tummy, then further. His fingers turned toward the floor before sliding between my legs. I felt his fingers glide over my wet sex.

"Ohhhh." My head fell back as he entered me, stroking. It was my turn.

I backed against the desk so I could open my legs wider. "Lick me, Hunter."

His smile was quickly replaced by hunger as he dropped between my spread thighs. I knew what he was thinking—every time he tried to stay in control, I told him what to do. I wasn't sorry.

I felt his hot tongue work between my lips, licking up my middle. I leaned back until I was lying on his desk, my knees falling to the side. He sucked in my clit as his fingers stroked inside of me. He licked, unfurling the pleasure like a flower.

"Oh my—" My breath started coming in pants, shallow and fast. I gyrated up into his mouth, feeling those fingers speed up. Feeling the friction. "Oh God," I moaned, soaking it in. A knot in my stomach tightened, making my muscles flex. The pleasure built higher. He worked faster.

"Oh my—Oh my—Oh G—" An orgasm ripped through me, making my whole body vibrate. I groaned out my release, shaking.

He straightened and then scooped me up. I squealed and clutched his shiny shoulders. I licked up his neck until he stopped by the couch. He set me down gently and sat. He motioned me toward him. "Sit on my cock, Olivia."

"Yes, sir," I said as desire rushed through me again. I swung my legs to either side of his. Then slowed down. I wanted him so badly it was starting to hurt, but I wanted to make this last.

I angled my body until his tip just lightly trailed up my sex. His breath hitched. He clutched the cushions. "If you weren't carrying my baby, I would throw you on the ground and fuck you hard, Olivia," he ground out between clenched teeth. His hard cock was straining.

I paused. His idea was better than mine.

I would have to make him lose control.

I leaned toward him, our bodies close but not touching. I just barely ran my tongue along his bottom lip, breathing the same air. Feeling the space between us heat up. I rose up, letting his tip trace a blazing trail up my wetness again.

His head came forward to capture my lips, but I backed off, not letting him. I lowered, still so slow. His knuckles turned white. I stopped, lining him up with my opening. I lowered the tiniest amount. His tip put pressure on, threatening to go in.

His hips jerked up, making his head part my folds. I backed off and then licked his bottom lip, teasing. Heat pulsed through me in waves.

"Damn it, Olivia. Sit!" His hips swung up again, but I rose up, not letting him completely enter me.

His hands smacked my butt cheeks, giving me a jolt of pleasure. He rammed me downward, filling me up in one hard movement.

"Hmm, Hunter." My head fell back. I let my hand fall between my legs, trailing my fingers across my nub. He lifted me and pulled down, thrusting into me. "Yes!"

And then I was weightless. I clutched his shoulders as he swung me under him, my back on the couch. He was compromising, it seemed. He thrust into me again, sending shooting sparks of pleasure through me.

I moaned as I wrapped my legs around his waist. He rammed into me, hard and fast. I clutched his back, pushing up to meet his downward thrusts. Pleasure pounded into me, stealing my thoughts. Taking my control. I held on for dear life as the sensations dragged me under.

"Yes, Hunter!" I pulled his neck down to me, locking my lips onto his. His tongue entered my mouth. His body created friction within me that spiraled outward. Everything tightened. Turned to lava.

"Yes, Hunter. Oh God, yes!" I blasted apart, convulsing. I panted, holding him tight. Riding this orgasm with him.

When we'd calmed down, he gave me a long, slow kiss. He stared down into my eyes. "I love you. I'll take you to my mother's this weekend. No more hiding."

Chapter 14

———— ❧ ————

ON SATURDAY AFTERNOON I sat with Pat and Janelle in the front room, sipping a sparkling water and pretending not to feel nervous. I wasn't worried about me. I had a pretty good idea that Trisha was on board with our life choices, no matter how unorthodox they might be. She seemed to like me, too, which was a fantastic bonus. What had been getting to me was how increasingly distant Hunter had become throughout the week until he barely talked to me or anyone else today. He'd gone into work late, spent time with the new hire, come home to get ready, and then locked himself in his study.

"This is the showdown, huh?" Janelle asked in her naturally quiet voice.

"What's his worry again?" Pat asked. She'd just finished making me up so I looked perfect for the future mother-in-law. I loved any excuse for her to come and do my hair and makeup.

"I think he's just thinking about the past." I chewed

my lip.

"Stop it, you'll ruin your lipstick," Pat said, leaning forward to check my face.

"Sorry." I rested my hand on my belly. "He keeps rubbing my stomach with a worried face. I think this meeting with his mom is messing with his head. He's dealing with all the old pain."

"So...he buried the pain in the past, didn't deal with it, and now all the ghosts are exploding out of the closet?" Pat's mouth formed an upside-down smile. I'd come to realize that this was her thinking face, not a frown. "That's no fun."

Or maybe it was a frown.

"Pretty much. I'm not Dr. Phil or anything, but this seems pretty cut and dry." I chewed on my nail. Pat sat forward and slapped my hand away from my face. "Sorry."

"But he does know that that baby is yours, right?" Janelle asked. "He's stopped being wishy-washy about that?"

"Of course it's hers..." Pat scowled at Janelle.

Janelle rolled her eyes. "Duh! Sorry, I meant he knows it's *his*."

"I think that's what is keeping him sane. He rubs my belly for comfort."

"He should've gone to a shrink." Pat sipped her sparkling wine. Just because I couldn't drink didn't mean she couldn't. At least, that was what she'd said when she opened the bottle.

"I think he did, but it didn't help all that much." I wiped some lint off my dress. "He's a tough nut to crack."

"You did it." Pat winked at me.

"I have no idea how."

Heavy footsteps sounded down the hall. Janelle sat forward, suddenly tense even though she wasn't on duty. Hunter made her nervous. But then, he made almost everyone nervous. Except Pat, who leaned just that little bit more into the chair and sipped her drink. Her job was done.

Hunter emerged with hard eyes and squared shoulders. He glanced at me, took in the other two, and crossed toward the door. Once there, he took his coat from the coat rack, and then mine. He paused, looking back at me. "Did you want this jacket, or another one?"

"That one is fine. Are you ready?" I heaved myself off the couch. My center of gravity was already starting to shift.

He walked back toward me, ignoring the ladies. "Yes. Let's go."

Pat frowned. I knew what she was thinking. His tone was curt and intense, his classic business persona meant to keep everyone at an arm's reach. He didn't usually use it with me. It might be a long evening.

I mouthed "Bye!" to the ladies and followed after him, quiet as a mouse. I was content to let him lead, and speak when spoken to. It was safer. I didn't know what lurked beneath these waters.

Hunter opened the Land Rover passenger door, helped me in, and then crossed to his side. Once we were on our way, his hand came to rest on my belly.

"How are you doing?" Clearly I wasn't great at only speaking when spoken to.

"Fine."

"I know. But really, how are you doing? I won't tell anyone, honest."

We stopped at a light. He looked out his window. "I know everything is fine, but I can't help my gut pinching. I keep thinking we're going to get there and you'll tell me you're leaving me and it's not my kid. I keep remembering how fucking shitty this all felt the first time around. I hate it. I hate feeling it."

It wasn't like Hunter to swear like that. Telling me to fuck him, sure. But this was more vulgar, somehow. He was using the harsher words to better define his pain.

I put my hand on his where it rested on my stomach, and for the first time, I finally understood. If I lost this baby, and Hunter with it, it would create a deep and profound wound that might never heal. I'd be in misery. My world would bleed of color and I would probably do anything to escape the pain, including burying myself so deep in my work that I could never feel emotion again.

I rubbed his hand. "I'm sorry you went through that."

He looked over at me, the sorrow haunting his gaze. A ghost of a smile touched his lips before he looked back at the road where the light had turned green. "I'll get through it. I'm just worried there is more pain to come. I don't really want to deal with it."

"I hear you. Every year on the anniversary of my father's death, it's like the scab is ripped off. It's a hard day. I keep thinking it'll dull, but so far, it hasn't."

"This dulled. After you came, the ache dulled. It had almost gone away…"

"And then I forced your mother on you."

"She blindsided you. I think it's the other way around."

It was true, but I was trying to be nice.

We spent the rest of the ride in silence. The closer we got, the more agitated Hunter became, until we pulled up right outside. His palm was sweaty where it rested on my stomach. He turned off the car and just sat for a minute. I sat with him, trying again for the fieldmouse thing.

"Tell me you're not going to leave me, Olivia. That you won't take my baby from me."

"No way would I! You can't get rid of me even if you wanted to. Seriously. I'd hunt you down for child support if nothing else."

Hunter huffed out a laugh, looking out the window with unfocused eyes. He thought I was kidding.

After another quiet moment, he heaved a big sigh and took the keys from the ignition. "Let's face the music."

He guided me up the walk and knocked on the door. It was only four o'clock in the afternoon. This was a garden party. I would've called it a BBQ, but I suspected I'd be the only one in this crowd that would.

"How many did she invite?" I asked.

"She said just a few from the neighborhood—whoever was available."

"When did you call her?"

"Wednesday."

The door opened slowly to reveal the oldest butler in the world. Father Time had nothing on this guy. And Death was probably pissed that this butler refused to come when called. Wrinkles swathed his face and gray hair grew in patches on his head.

"Mr. Carlisle, Miss Jonston, welcome." He stepped back with a pompous air to admit us.

I had no idea why, but I freaking loved this butler. He was such a character, whether he realized it or not.

"Hello, Mr. Smith," Hunter responded dutifully, if in a harsh tone, and directed me inside. Hunter's whole body was tense. I shifted from side to side with nervous energy. Mr. Smith turned back to us and led us through the somewhat dated house. It was still elegant, though, and handsomely furnished. We went to the backyard, where Mr. Smith left us with a "Here you go, sir. Miss."

"Thank you, Mr. Smith." Hunter directed me outside. The soft sunshine from the late afternoon sprinkled over a backyard with a pool, lawn chairs, and a patio.

"She has a pool?" I asked with a wispy voice. Just my luck I realized this *after* I'd gotten pregnant. I had a feeling that bathing suits would be the devil for a while.

"Hey!" Mike, the construction guy, stepped forward with a crater of a smile. "Look at you!" He put out his hand to me.

With a red face, I shook his hand. "Hi."

"You are absolutely glowing. Congratulations!" He offered his hand to Hunter next, his smile turning up in wattage. "Here's the lucky papa."

Hunter's lips tweaked, a smile threatening his previous scowl. His eyes started to glimmer as an older lady came up with a delighted smile. "Oh, how exciting! My daughter refuses to have children, and my son is hopeless. He just can't find a girl to save his life. I can't wait to hold him or her—do you know what it is yet?"

"In a couple weeks," I said demurely.

"Now, give them some space." Trisha walked up with poise and grace, as always, but I could see the hustle in her step. The anxiousness. She smiled at me before coming to stand directly in front of Hunter. Her smile increased as her eyes turned glossy. She held out her arms for a hug.

A quick look of shock passed over Hunter's face. He paused for a moment.

"Well, c'mon," Mike boomed, clapping Hunter on the back. "Give your mother a hug. She tries to hide it, but she is over the moon. She probably dances around when no one is watching. She's told everyone in the neighborhood."

"Oh, now!" The older lady slapped Mike playfully, beaming at me.

As Hunter stepped forward to hug his mother, a boyish look crossed his face. She clung to him for a moment, patting his shoulder softly. When they each stepped back, she took out a tissue from her pocket and dabbed her eye.

"Come in, come in," Trisha said, falling to my side and looping her arm around mine.

I knew this trick—she was kidnapping me. And just like she had probably planned, Hunter followed along immediately, clearly not wanting his precious cargo to have any distance from him on this excursion.

"There's no need to dwell on the past, Hunter," his mom said softly. "What happened then doesn't matter. That was a different time and you were a different person." She stopped us in front of a bar on wheels. There was no tiki bar for this house. And I'd been right—even though there was a BBQ smoking, this party could not be called something so mundane.

"You've opened up lately in a way I haven't seen since before…your late teens." She tapped my arm. "You have a loving fiancée and you'll be an excellent father. Don't let what happened when you were young and naive dim what is happening now. Olivia doesn't deserve it."

She patted my belly and turned to me. Her eyes connected with mine solemnly. "Thank you for pushing my son on this path. I'm lucky he found you. You've given me my boy back." Her eyes teared up and her mouth started quivering. "Excuse me." She put her hand to her mouth and turned away elegantly, walking out of sight.

Hunter's arm came around my waist. He pulled me close. He didn't say a word. And then he couldn't if he tried.

"You are a *ravishing* mother-to-be!" A woman I vaguely recognized came over, causing a flock of other older ladies to crowd around.

"This is so exciting," another woman exclaimed.

"Congratulations." A man thrust a hand in Hunter's direction. A random hand found its way to my stomach, followed by another.

Hunter might be burying his demons, but this was creating a host of them for me. I didn't necessarily like being touched by strangers, and I *definitely* didn't like being ganged up on and group-touched. There was something incredibly wrong about random hands roving over my stomach.

I tried my best to keep a smile and not wriggle away.

After we got our drinks—I went with a sparkling apple cider to look like a joiner—Hunter escorted me to some seats near the pool. Thankfully, after I sat the buzzards stopped circling. Instead, they settled near us, smiling all the time. If this were a children's party, we'd be the clowns. All these people were apparently waiting for us to do a trick.

"So you went and started a business, huh?" Mike asked, pulling over a chair.

"Oh, really?" a woman asked. She leaned forward to catch every last detail, practically in my lap now.

I was starting to get uncomfortable with all the closeness.

"Livy was kind enough to let me in on her business venture," Hunter said. He rested a hand on the arm of my chair. His shoulders had completely relaxed, as had his bearing.

I scoffed. "He was in on it from the beginning, he just didn't tell me until someone else ousted him."

"And is it doing well?" Mike asked with a knowing gleam to his eye.

"We're coming along," Hunter said with a streak of modesty.

"Who is this guy?" I asked, giving Hunter an evil grin. "Since when are you coy about your achievements?"

Trisha came cover to stand behind Mike. Three men, Hunter and Mike included, jumped up and offered their seats. Trisha waved them away. "I have another guest arriving. I need to stay mobile. Sit, sit!"

"I can't sit with you standing." Mike put a hand on her back and one on his chair. "Take this one. Please."

"Oh!" She allowed herself to take the chair and then rested her hands elegantly in her lap.

I felt like such a barbarian when she was around.

"He's magic," Mike said, crossing his arms. "Didn't I tell you? He touches a business and it takes off."

"Olivia and Bruce are doing the hard work," Hunter explained, a fire coming to his eyes I'd never seen when he was talking about his old job. "They've created a product that is as easy to sell as feeding cake to children.

All the elements are there, I just had to structure it right and set it in motion."

"You did much more than that." Trisha gave Hunter a proud smile. "I did a general search for the game and I got all sorts of links right away. That game is everywhere. That isn't usual, I don't think."

"We marketed it pretty hard to get it in people's hands. After that, word of mouth spread like wildfire." Hunter let a smile blossom, the first since he'd been here. He showered me with that sexy, smoldering gaze. "I have a great partner."

A couple of the women said, "Aww."

"So how did he propose?" a woman with a giant purple hat asked me. Thus began the second leg of the garden party—the question and answer segment. I was asked to recall, in detail, the whole day of Hunter proposing. I left out my mother, but the gasps of delight and the teary eyes after telling them about Hunter asking my father was crazy. Even the guys were impressed. Mike noted that Hunter was smart in more than just business.

Hunter didn't talk much, allowing me to get harangued without interference, but he never checked out, either. He listened to all my answers, not allowing the men to pull him away. He scooted his chair as close to me as possible, and occasionally laid his hand on my belly. Occasionally, because whenever he did it, someone else wanted to join in on the fun. Finally I had to give him death threats within my looks so he would stop.

An hour or so in, the door opened again and I heard

the butler's droll voice. I glanced up, and then choked on my drink.

My mom stood in the doorway.

"Oh great, let's make this afternoon super awkward." I glared at Hunter.

His brow furrowed. Until he saw what the problem was. "I didn't invite her."

Trisha walked over to my mom and escorted her toward us.

"I need to tell you something," Hunter said softly.

I didn't like the sound of that. "Now?"

He hesitated. "Maybe we should meet her first. Welcome her here."

"Probably, if only to tell her that she needs to be nice."

He helped me up, then directed me to meet her in the middle. She smiled when I saw her, strangely loose-limbed and actually...happy. Did she get a prescription for Prozac or was she faking really well?

"Hey, Mom," I said through a tight jaw. I had tension enough for the both of us.

"I thought it might be nice for your relatives to be here as well." Trisha gave me a kind smile. She had no idea what havoc she was wreaking. My mom could kill a party if a bad mood struck her. Not that I could tell the perfect hostess all of that, of course. So I smiled and thanked her, relieved when she moved away.

"Mom, I can't have you embarrassing me here," I said as quietly as I could while keeping a smile on my face.

A glimmer of regret rolled through her expression. She waved me away. "I know how to act at an influential party, Olivia. I've been to more than a few."

I glanced at Hunter, incredibly embarrassed about what was coming next. There was nothing for it, though. It had to be said. "You cannot hit on any of these men. Even the single ones. It's not that kind of party."

My mom rolled her eyes. She glanced at Hunter for a moment before schooling her expression into one of chastisement. "I know the rules."

"Rules?" I said.

She glanced at Hunter again. Wariness crossed her features this time. A hint of desperation tinged her voice. "You didn't tell her?"

"Not yet. I've had…other things on my mind."

"Tell me what?" I asked Hunter.

"I've put your mother on an allowance. She will be more than taken care of, allowing that she follow a certain list of…guidelines."

"Rules." She gave me a winning smile. That one was definitely fake, bordering on condescending.

"Among them are who she sees—"

"No married men, he means," my mom said in a scratchy, annoyed voice. "I'm perfectly happy forgoing men entirely. You don't have to worry."

I shook my head, mystified. "What else?"

"It doesn't matter," Hunter said, command slipping into his voice.

My mom squinted at Hunter, her stubborn streak showing. She didn't like to be told what to do, and that voice probably reminded her of times when she had to. In this, I agreed.

"It *does* matter, because this concerns me." I braced my hands on my hips.

"I'll just let you two work it out. Let me know if I've been cut off." My mom raised her chin and sauntered away. The tension was back in her frame. I actually hadn't noticed it until it was absent. And things clicked into place. Hunter had been right—she'd been desperate all those years with no money. She latched on to anyone she could, trying to find some security. For a brief moment when she walked into this backyard, she'd had it. For the first time in her life, probably, she didn't have to worry. She didn't have a kid to take care of, and she had a steady stream of money coming in.

"This isn't your problem, Hunter," I said, somewhat miserably. If anyone should be supporting her, it should be me. And I could probably swing it, so I should.

"You're my wife in practice if not in name, Olivia. She is unhappy, and therefore makes those around her unhappy. I changed that variable, that's all."

"How much are you giving her?"

"Mostly, I made her put me in charge of her finances. Large purchases will need to go through me, and any frivolous expenditure over a dollar limit. Her allowance from me is surprisingly little. It was more a matter of capitalizing on her investments, or in some cases, investing properly."

"And how did this come about?" I was really trying to be angry, because logically, this had crossed the line. The thing was, I should've done it. I should've known all this, and forced my way to help. I didn't have his golden thumb, but I could've helped support her. I said as much.

"No." He shook his head and led me away from a few ladies who were creeping into our space. They probably wanted more time touching my stomach. I was going to have to try and rig a bug zapper to fend them off. "She would've squandered it. She is remarkably bad with money. She needed a strong hand to guide her. You're too…lenient."

"Nice way of putting it." I couldn't help a sardonic laugh. I let the woman walk all over me, and he knew it. "So what are the rules?"

"Just the spending issues, her dating habits…" He trailed away, but I knew him well enough to know he was omitting.

"What else?"

"I want our child to know both sides of grandparents, except for my father. I've given her guidelines regarding how she treats those around her."

"You're forcing her to be nice?"

A smile touched his lips before he bent down to kiss me. "My job is to protect you, and that includes your mother's bad moods."

I laughed, snaking my arms around his middle.

"Serves her right."

"I thought so. But it doesn't seem like she'll need it. I didn't expect a genuine smile when she was in our presence."

"You noticed! I didn't know *what* to think." I hugged him tight, relishing his arms coming around my back.

"You aren't mad?"

I shrugged. "Like I said, I can't be. I basically do whatever your mother says, and you make my mother do whatever you say. Your family is dominating mine. I think my mother and I have both realized it's just easier to let the Carlisles have their way. It works to our benefit in the end."

"Soon you'll be a Carlisle. Listen, Livy, I wondered...I realize you want the big wedding when your body is back to...your own—"

"Nice save."

"—what do you think about legalizing it now? We wouldn't have to tell anyone, but...I'd like to be married to you when the baby comes. I want you to think like I do, and you won't until it's official. So let's make it official. After the baby we can do a big event."

"Make it official, like...when?"

"As soon as we can get a license. Today if you want."

"I doubt any government offices are open past five." I put a hand on my chest to stop my heart from trying to explode out of my ribcage. Suddenly I couldn't breathe.

"I can arrange it if you don't mind getting married

by a judge…"

"Oh my God." I took deep breaths. A wave of excitement I didn't realize I'd been suppressing crashed down onto me. He was serious. He wanted to marry me *right now*. I could become Mrs. Carlisle today.

I looked up into those sexy brown eyes and fell in. The answer came naturally. "Yes."

Chapter 15

HUNTER AND I stood in a patch of grass with the garden party spread out behind us. In front of us was Tim, Trisha's friend and a judge. He could marry people. And was, *right now.*

I was jittery and excited and happy and on the verge of tears as I faced Hunter. What was better—my mom was sporting a genuine smile again. As soon as she'd heard Hunter would continue to ensure she was taken care of, she had a green light for happiness.

"Dearly beloved, we are gathered here today to join Olivia Jonston and Hunter Carlisle in matrimony..." Tim squinted down at the piece of paper he was reading. He'd actually never married anyone before and had no idea what to do or say.

It didn't matter. Nothing mattered but the man standing in front of me.

As the words of forever drifted around us, I fell into Hunter's eyes, full of love and longing, of joy and support. When the time came, I gave him my hand so he could slip his grandmother's wedding ring onto my finger, a circle made of diamonds. It was something Trisha hadn't offered Hunter when he'd proposed to Denise all those many years ago. We were breaking the mold of his past. The last weight pressing down on him was being lifted.

Hunter's ring had been purchased an hour before from the nearest jewelry store still open. I slipped it on his finger, cherishing his smile and look of devotion. It was happening. I was marrying Hunter Carlisle!

"Will you, Olivia Jonston…take Hunter Carlisle to be your awfully wedded—sorry! *Law*fully wedded wife. Dang it. Husband! The ink is smudged right there, I apologize." Tim took a deep breath and tried again. "Will you, Olivia Jonston, take Hunter Carlisle to be your lawfully wedded husband, to have and to hold, through sickness and in health, till death do you part?"

"I do," I said, laughing through happy tears.

"Hunter Carlisle, will you take Olivia Jonston to be your *law*fully wedded wife, to have and to hold, in sickness and in health, till death do you part?"

"Now he's got it," Mike rumbled. There was a smattering of laughter and sniffles both.

"I do," Hunter said softly.

"By the power vested in me, by the state of Indiana—California, sorry. It says the wrong state. By the state of California, I now declare you husband and wife." Tim sighed in relief and lowered his paper. I laughed again.

"Kiss the bride!" someone shouted.

"What?" Tim brought the paper back up.

"Tell him to kiss the bride!" people shouted.

"Oh right, right." Tim wiped his forehead. "You may kiss the bride!"

Hunter put his hand to my chin as everyone clapped and whistled, and leaned into me. Our lips connected, soft and sweet, his first kiss as my husband.

"I love you, Olivia," Hunter said softly.

"I love you."

He kissed me again before throwing an arm over my shoulder and smiling at the crowd of onlookers. Champagne popped and people cheered, our family as happy as we were. Today was the first day of the rest of my life, and I couldn't wait for the days to come.

Epilogue

───※───

I STEPPED OUTSIDE and let the Napa Valley sun rain down on me. I had a tray in my hand full of cheeses and my body was almost back to normal. It had been one year to the day since I gave birth to my healthy baby boy. He was big at eight pounds, one ounce, with little baby rolls on his thighs and arms. My mom suggested we name him Hunter. Thankfully, Hunter was the first to say no to the idea, preferring he had his own identity.

I took the plate to the table set up on the patio. We'd decided to have little Brandon's birthday at our Napa Valley estate, since it had plenty of rooms for visitors to stay, not to mention we stayed here most often these days.

"Do you need help?" Kimberly asked. She was sporting her shiny diamond ring with her own wedding only a couple of months away.

Hunter had talked to Robby like he said he would, and it turned out, Robby already had a ring. He just couldn't settle on a way to ask. He'd put so much pressure on himself that he repeatedly talked himself out of the whole situation. All it took was one brainstorming session with me and the assurance she'd say yes, and he was off to the races.

Speaking of weddings...I really needed to get on that. Or at least a reception. But really, it was just a few friends that hadn't witnessed the event, and all but Kimberly hated weddings anyway. What was the point? Everyone would know the white dress was a sham—I already had a kid! And a husband!

"No, Kimmie, I'm fine. We have the caterers—I was just bringing this out since I was on my way. Trisha will probably scold me for it."

"Hey, baby," Hunter said as he slipped his hand around my waist.

I leaned into his warmth. It was sunny, but it wasn't summer. There was still a decided chill to the air, and Hunter's heat cut right through it. I angled my face up. He bent to plant a soft kiss on my lips. Together we watched my mom slowly saunter behind Brandon with a glass of wine in her hand.

"I cannot believe he's walking already," Kimberly said. As she said it, Brandon tumbled in a heap of little legs and arms. Undeterred, he started crawling across the grass. My mom kept stride.

"Livy, honey..." Trisha, the real organizer of this party, walked up to us. "It's time to cut the cake. I've started to gather everyone." She gestured toward the far table where the face painter was moving out of the way.

We followed her over, moving to stand beside Bert's huge girth. I didn't get to see him much anymore because we didn't have a commute with our office being our laptops, and we weren't in the city much. Our company was going strong—stronger than even Hunter had anticipated. We were bringing in large amounts of money, had a solid fan base, and kept producing games that ranked high and had great reviews. We'd just launched our first "world," where people could compete across country lines. So far, so good.

Hunter had kept his promise. He worked less than forty hours, and spent all the time he could with his son. He was every bit the great dad he wanted to be, kind and patient, and always loving. While he might keep the world at bay, he never distanced himself from Brandon or me. He doled out plenty of hugs, kisses, and I-love-yous.

"Where's the birthday boy?" Bert bent down to his wife, a short, petite little thing that defied logic when it came to match-ups. She pointed to the grass where my mother was trying to wrangle a crying baby. It wasn't easy with the glass of wine.

"Oh shoot," I said, starting off in that direction.

"I'll get him!" Bert jogged over, bending down to scoop him up. Brandon squealed with laughter as Bert held him out like an airplane, flying through the sky.

"Let's get that cake divided up. Looks delicious." Brenda sipped a glass of red wine. I didn't realize she drank anything other than coffee.

Bert handed Brandon to Hunter, and I took a moment to marvel how alike the two were. Brandon was the spitting image of his daddy, except his eyes were lighter like mine. There could be absolutely no doubt whose son he was.

I smiled and snuggled into them. Hunter hefted Brandon into one arm, and encircled me with the other, while the caterers finished setting up.

We'd had a large package delivered that morning from an anonymous source. Within the package was a giant bundle of toys, and an account in Brandon's name with a hundred thousand dollars in it, due when Brandon turned eighteen. The postmark was two miles away from Rodge's house. The account was set up by Rodge's office. He might not have gotten along with his son, but Rodge was trying to take care of his grandson. There was no way I'd allow the man access to my kid, but it had to be acknowledged that he was doing right by Brandon.

I closed my eyes for a moment of bliss as a swell of love filled me. That first yes had changed my life. Looking back, there were moments of pain, and some of sorrow, but I wouldn't change one single thing from the first moment I met Hunter. How it all worked out was perfection.

The End

Made in the USA
Lexington, KY
30 April 2016